HOW BEAUTIFUL THE ORDINARY

·

TWELVE STORIES OF IDENTITY

WRITTEN BY
MICHAEL CART:

WHAT'S SO FUNNY?:
Wit and Humor in American Children's Literature

FROM ROMANCE TO REALISM: 50 Years of Growth
and Change in Young Adult Literature

MY FATHER'S SCAR

THE HEART HAS ITS REASONS: Young Adult Literature
with Gay/Lesbian/Queer Content, 1969–2004
(with Christine A. Jenkins)

EDITED BY
MICHAEL CART

LOVE & SEX: Ten Stories of Truth

NECESSARY NOISE:
Stories About Our Families as They Really Are

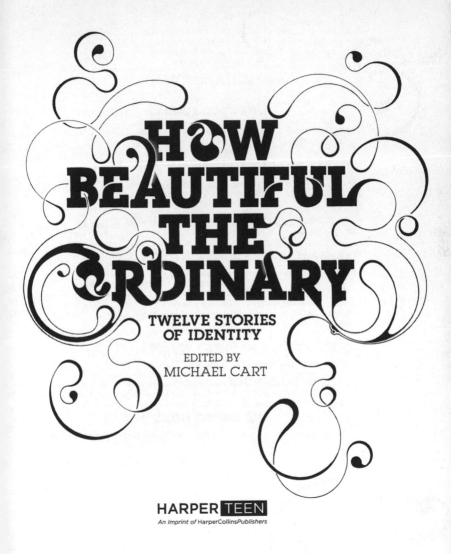

HOW BEAUTIFUL THE ORDINARY

TWELVE STORIES OF IDENTITY

EDITED BY
MICHAEL CART

HARPER TEEN
An Imprint of HarperCollins*Publishers*

HarperTeen is an imprint of HarperCollins Publishers.

How Beautiful the Ordinary: Twelve Stories of Identity
"A Word from the Nearly Distant Past" copyright © 2009 by David Levithan
"Happily Ever After" copyright © 2009 by Eric Shanower
"My Life as a Dog" copyright © 2009 by Ron Koertge
"Trev" copyright © 2009 by Jacqueline Woodson
"My Virtual World" copyright © 2009 by Francesca Lia Block
"A Dark Red Love Knot" copyright © 2009 by Margo Lanagan
"Fingernail" copyright © 2009 by William Sleator
"Dyke March" copyright © 2009 by Ariel Schrag
"The Missing Person" copyright © 2009 by Jennifer Finney Boylan
"First Time" copyright © 2009 by Julie Ann Peters
"Dear Lang" copyright © 2009 by Emma Donoghue
"The Silk Road Runs through Tupperneck, N.H." copyright © 2009 by Gregory Maguire
All rights reserved. Printed in the United States of America. No part of this book
may be used or reproduced in any manner whatsoever without written permission
except in the case of brief quotations embodied in critical articles and reviews. For
information address HarperCollins Children's Books, a division of HarperCollins
Publishers, 10 East 53rd Street, New York, NY 10022.
www.harperteen.com

Library of Congress Cataloging-in-Publication Data
How beautiful the ordinary : twelve stories of identity / edited by Michael Cart. — 1st ed.
    v. cm.
    Summary: Presents twelve stories by contemporary, award-winning young adult authors,
some presented in graphic or letter format, which explore themes of gender identity, love,
and sexuality.
    Contents: A word from the nearly distant past / David Levithan — Happily ever
after / Eric Shanower — My life as a dog / Ron Koertge — Trev / Jacqueline Woodson
— My virtual world / Francesca Lia Block — A dark red love knot / Margo Lanagan
— Fingernail / William Sleator — Dyke March / Ariel Schrag — The missing person
/ Jennifer Finney Boylan — First time / Julie Anne Peters — Dear Lang / Emma
Donoghue — The Silk Road runs through Tupperneck, N.H. / Gregory Maguire.
    ISBN 978-0-06-115498-0
    1. Short stories, American. 2. Gender identity—Juvenile fiction. [1. Short stories. 2.
Sexual orientation—Fiction. 3. Identity—Fiction. 4. Homosexuality—Fiction. 5. Sex—
Fiction. 6. Love—Fiction.] I. Cart, Michael.
PZ5.H7793 2009   2008051769
[Fic]—dc22   CIP
                                                                        AC

09 10 11 12 13   CG/RRDB   10 9 8 7 6 5 4 3 2 1
❖
First Edition

HOW
BEAUTIFUL
THE
ORDINARY

·

TWELVE STORIES
OF IDENTITY

CONTENTS

•

STORIES OF IDENTITY

There are countless reasons for reading, but when you're young and uncertain of your identity, of who you may be, one of the most compelling is the quest to discover yourself reflected in the pages of a book. What a comfort *that* provides, seeing that you are not alone, that you are not—as you had feared—the only one of your kind. But what if you search whole libraries of such books in vain for your own face? That—for too many years—was the plight of gay, lesbian, and transgender young adults. For as far as literature was concerned, they were invisible. And even when gay and lesbian characters did begin appearing in the late 1960s and early 1970s, they were too often presented—stereotypically—as unhappy outsiders doomed to lives lived as "the other" on the outer fringes of society. Transgender teens remained invisible even longer, for their faces didn't appear in fiction for young adults until 2004. And they remain among the most underrepresented—and least understood—people in all of literature.

Which suggests another compelling reason for reading: It's a wonderful opportunity to meet those who may—in whatever way—be different from us. By taking us into characters' minds, hearts, and lives, literature has an uncanny ability to help us understand that those we previously regarded as "the other" are—in terms of our common humanity—actually "us."

In this spirit it's fortunate that in the last decade or so an increasingly large body of such literature has finally begun accruing. It now offers not only honest but also artful portrayals of lesbian, gay, and transgender young adults. As a result, these lives are being made accessible to *all* readers.

This collection contains stories by twelve of our finest authors for young adults, writing about what it might mean to be gay, lesbian, or transgender. Whether you're transgender, gay, or straight, you will find your own meanings in the stories that follow, of course, but for me one area of commonality is . . . their *un*commonality. For, we discover, gay, lesbian, and transgender lives are as wonderfully various, diverse, and gloriously complex as any other lives. And not only are the *lives* these authors depict varied, so also are the strategies and devices they have used to tell their stories. As they demonstrate, while we can still find the truth of human experience in works of realism, we can also find it in works of speculative fiction; we can find it in traditional stories but also in nontraditional narratives; we can find it in words but also in pictures. Consider the contents of the book you're about to read.

It begins with David Levithan's nontraditional story, which is addressed directly to the reader; it's a story that, with singular sweetness, examines the present and future lives of a half-dozen gay teenagers as they—and the reader—find a nearly perfect balance between the past and the future that promises to produce an attainable world of fulfillment and heartsease.

If that sounds almost magical, the next story contains elements of real magic as award-winning cartoonist Eric Shanower creates a graphic story about a troubled relationship that is complicated by the intervention of a genie who might have strayed into the story from the pages of *The Arabian Nights*. It turns out there's magic not only in brass bottles but also in love.

Novelist and poet Ron Koertge then delivers a quirky work of experimental fiction that is rooted in the dangers and difficulties of coming out—still an issue even for today's gay teens—and how one young man finds and frees himself in a totally unexpected and wonderfully imaginative way.

Next, Jacqueline Woodson, winner of the Margaret A. Edwards Award, takes us inside the mind and heart of Trev, a young girl who knows what the rest of the world can't—that she's really a boy—and then shows us how he struggles heroically—even *super*heroically—to come to terms with his true self.

Francesca Lia Block, another Margaret A. Edwards Award winner, writes a haunting and lyrical story that begins in a virtual world when two young people encounter each other online and then develop a heartfelt relationship that will result in surprise . . . and satisfaction.

Australian author and two-time winner of the Michael L. Printz Honor Award Margo Lanagan finds inspiration for her gorgeously written story of not one but two desperate encounters with love in the classic poem "The Highwayman." Prepare to be dazzled.

William Sleator, that master of the outré, turns not to literature but to Thailand for his realistic and moving story of a young Thai man's hazardous quest to find love, but in the wrong place, face, and arms.

Then the gifted young cartoonist Ariel Schrag, whose graphic novels *Awkward*, *Dysfunction*, *Potential*, and *Likewise* chronicled her four years at Berkeley High School, offers readers a hilarious, sometimes existential, occasionally delusional tourist's-eye view of a San Francisco dyke march. (Get your picture taken with a topless dancer!)

Jennifer Finney Boylan, author of the bestselling memoir *She's Not There: A Life in Two Genders*, writes a story about a girl who vanishes and the summer when a young teen named Jimmy "gave up on being a boy and became a girl instead."

Julie Anne Peters is a boundary breaker. Her novel *Luna*, a National Book Award finalist, was the first YA novel to feature a transgender character. Now in her story "First Time" she writes tenderly and honestly about two teenage girls who make the difficult—and occasionally terrifying—decision to express their love for each other physically.

In "Dear Lang," Emma Donoghue offers a short

story in the form of a heartfelt letter from a forgotten mother to the teenage daughter whom she hasn't seen in fourteen years.

And Gregory Maguire writes a story that, moving backward and forward in time, introduces readers to a man who confronts his memories of a passionate but "accidental" romance that still resonates in his present-day life.

And there you have it: twelve stories—alike only in the wonderful variety of their subjects, styles, and structures—that dramatically demonstrate that lesbian, gay, and transgender lives are extraordinary, yes, but also *ordinary.* How beautiful!

Michael Cart

A WORD FROM THE
NEARLY DISTANT PAST

·

BY DAVID LEVITHAN

You can't know what it is like for us now—you will always be one step behind.

Be thankful for that.

You can't know what it was like for us then—you will always be one step ahead.

Be thankful for that, too.

Trust us: There is a nearly perfect balance between the past and the future. As we become the distant past, you become a future only a few of us would have imagined.

It's hard to think of such things when you are busy dreaming or loving or screwing. The context falls away. We are a spirit-burden you carry, like that of your grandparents, or friends who moved away. We try to make it as light a burden as possible. We cannot be escapist in the same way. When we see you, there is nothing but context. We apologize: We cannot see you without thinking of ourselves. We were once the ones who were dreaming and loving and screwing. We were the ones who were living, and then we were the ones who were dying. We sewed ourselves, a thread's width, into your history. The generation of like-loving souls that was cut down before you were born.

We were once like you, only our world wasn't like yours.

You have no idea how close to death you came. Ten years. Twenty years. A generation or two earlier, you might not be here with us.

We resent you. You astonish us.

It's 8:07 P.M. on Saturday, March 8, and right now Neil Hayden is thinking of us. He is fifteen, and he is walking over to his boyfriend Peter's house. They have been going out for a year, and Neil starts by thinking about how long this seems. From the beginning, everyone has been telling him how it won't last. But now, even if it doesn't last forever, it feels like it has lasted long enough to be something. Peter's parents treat Neil like a second son, and while his own parents are still alternately confused and distressed, they haven't barred any of the doors.

Neil has a DVD, two bottles of Diet Dr Pepper,

cookie dough, and a book of Mark Doty poems in his backpack. This—and Peter—is all it takes for him to feel profoundly lucky. But luck, we've learned, is actually part of an invisible equation. Two blocks away from Peter's house, Neil gets a glimpse of this, and is struck with a feeling of deep, unnamed gratitude. He realizes that part of his good fortune is his place in history, and he thinks fleetingly of us, the ones who came before. We are not names or faces to him; we are an abstraction, a force. His gratitude is a rare thing—it is much more likely for a boy to feel thankful for the Diet Dr Pepper than he is to feel thankful for being healthy and alive, for being able to walk to his boyfriend's house at age fifteen without any doubt that this is the right thing to do.

He has no idea how beautiful he is as he walks up that path and rings that doorbell. He has no idea how beautiful the ordinary becomes once it disappears.

If you are a teenager now, it's unlikely that you knew us well. We are your shadow uncles, your angel godfathers, your mother's best friend from college, the author of the book you found in the gay section of the library. We are characters in a Tony Kushner play; we are names on a quilt that rarely gets taken out anymore. We are the ghosts of the remaining older generation. You know some of our songs.

We do not want to haunt you too somberly. We don't want our legacy to be *gravitas*. You wouldn't want to live your life like that, and you won't want to be remembered like that, either. Your mistake would be to find our commonality in our dying. The living part mattered more.

We taught you how to dance.

It's true. Look at Erik Johnson on the dance floor. Seriously—look at him. Six feet tall, one hundred eighty pounds, all of which can be converted by the right clothes and the right song into a mass of heedless joy. (The right hair helps, too.) He treats his body like it's made of fireworks, each one timed to the beat. Is he dancing alone or dancing with everyone? Here's the secret: It doesn't matter. He traveled for two hours to get to the city, and when it's all over, it will take him over two hours to get home. But it's worth it. Freedom isn't just about voting and marrying and kissing on the street, although all of these things are important. Freedom is also about what you will allow yourself to do.

We watch Erik Johnson when he's sitting in Spanish class, sketching imaginary maps in his notebook. We watch Erik Johnson when he's sitting in the cafeteria, stealing glances at older boys. We watch Erik Johnson as he lays the clothes on his bed, creating an outline of the person he's going to be tonight. We spent years doing these things. But this was what we looked forward to, the thing that Erik looks forward to. This freedom.

Music isn't much different now from what it was when we hit the dance floor. This means something. We found something universal. We bottled that desire, then released it into airwaves. The sounds hit your body, and you move.

We are in those particles that send you. We are in that music.

Dance for us, Erik.

Feel us there in your freedom.

It was an exquisite irony: Just when we stopped wanting to kill ourselves, we started to die. Just when we were feeling strength, it was taken from us.

This should not happen to you.

Talk all you want about youth feeling invincible. Surely, some of us had that bravado. But there was also the dark inner voice telling us we were doomed. And then we were doomed. And then we weren't.

You should not feel doomed. Not in the same way.

You can only doom yourself.

"Let's just do it," one boy says to another.

We yell *no*.

And when we're not heard, it hurts even more.

We know that some of you are still scared. We know that some of you are still silent. Just because it's better now doesn't mean that it's good.

Dreaming and loving and screwing. None of these are really identities. Maybe when other people look at us, but not to ourselves. We are so much more complicated than that.

We wish we could offer you a creation myth, an exact reason why you are the way you are, why when you read this sentence, you will know it's about you. But we don't know how it began. We don't know how it will end. We barely understood the time that we knew.

You will miss the taste of Froot Loops.

You will miss the sound of traffic.

You will miss your back against his.

You will even miss him stealing the sheets.

Do not ignore these things.

At the risk of sounding old, we have to say: It's far too easy to get porn nowadays. We could drag out that first thrill—the quickly glanced magazine at the newsstand, the elaborately planned mail order—for years. Now it wears off in days. We're glad that it's less taboo. But how sad to deprive it of all mystery, to freight sex so early with explicit expectation.

Ricky Schiller, we see you. We're not above peeking over your shoulder.

Really, you need to get out more.

There are few things that can make us quite as happy as a gay prom.

Tonight we're in a town with the improbable name of Kindling—surely the pioneers had a fiery death wish. Somewhere along the way, someone must have learned the third little pig's lesson, since the community center is built entirely of bricks. It's a dull, quiet building in a dull, quiet town—its architecture as beautiful as the word *municipal*. It is an unlikely place for a blue-haired boy and a pink-haired boy to meet.

Kindling does not have enough gay kids to support a prom on its own. So tonight, the cars drive in from minutes—sometimes hours—away. Some of the couples drive in together, laughing or fighting or pausing in their separate silences. Some of the boys drive in alone—they've snuck out of the house, or they're meeting friends at the community center, or they saw the listing online and decided at the last minute to go. There are boys in tuxedos, boys adorned with flowers, boys wearing torn hoodies, boys in ties as skinny as their jeans, boys in ironic taffeta gowns, boys in unironic taffeta gowns, boys in V-neck T-shirts, boys who feel awkward wearing dress shoes. And girls—girls wearing all these things, driving to the same place.

If we went to our proms, we went with girls. Some of us had a good time; some of us looked back years later and wondered how we had managed to be so oblivious to ourselves. A few of us managed to go with each other, with our best female friends covering as our dates. We were invited to this ritual, but only if we maintained a socially sanctioned fiction. It would have been more likely for Neil Armstrong to invite us to a prom on the moon than it was for us to go to a prom like the one being held in Kindling tonight.

When we were in high school, hair existed on the bland spectrum of black/brown/orange/blond/gray/white. But tonight in Kindling we have Ryan walking into the community center with his hair dyed a robin's-egg blue. Ten minutes later, Avery walks in with his hair the color of a Mary Kay Cadillac. Ryan's hair is spiked like the surface of a rocky ocean, while Avery's swoops gently over his eyes. Ryan is from Kindling and Avery is from Marigold, a town forty miles away. We can tell immediately that they've never met, and that they are going to.

We are not unanimous about the hair. Some of us think it is ridiculous to have blue hair or pink hair. Others of us wish we could go back and make our hair mimic the Jell-O our mothers would serve us in the afternoon.

We are rarely unanimous about anything. Some of us loved. Some of us were in love. Some of us were loved. Some of us never understood what the fuss was about. Some of us wanted it so badly that we died trying. Some of us swear we died of heartbreak, not AIDS.

Ryan walks into the prom, and then Avery walks in ten minutes later. We know what's going to happen. We have seen this scene so many times before. We just don't know if it will work, or if it will last.

We think of the boys we kissed, the boys we screwed, the boys we loved, the boys who didn't love us back, the boys who were with us at the end, the boys who were with us beyond the end. Love is so painful, how could you ever wish it on anybody? And love is so essential, how could you ever stand in its way?

Ryan and Avery do not see us. They do not know us, or need us, or feel us in the room. They don't even see each other until about twenty minutes into the prom. Ryan sees Avery over the head of a thirteen-year-old boy in (it's true, so gay) rainbow suspenders. He spots Avery's hair first, then Avery. And Avery looks up at just that moment, and sees the blue-haired boy glancing his way.

Some of us applaud. Others look away, because it hurts too much.

We always underestimated our own participation in magic. That is, we thought of magic as something inherent, something that existed with or without us. But that's simply not true. Things are not magical because they've been conjured or created for us by some outside force. They are magical because we create them and then deem them so. Ryan and Avery will say the first moment they spoke, the first moment they danced, was magical. But they were the ones—no one else, nothing else—who gave it the magic. We know. We were there. Ryan opened himself to it. Avery opened himself to it. And the act of opening was all they needed. *That* is the magic.

Focus in. The blue-haired boy leads. He smiles as he takes the pink-haired boy's hand. He feels what we know: The supernatural is natural; wonderment can come from the most mundane satisfaction, like a heartbeat or a glance. And the pink-haired boy is scared, so incredibly scared—only the thing you've most wished for can scare you in that way. Hear their heartbeats. Listen close.

Now draw back. See the other kids on the dance floor. The comfortable misfits, the torn rebels, the fearful and the brave. Dancing or not dancing. Talking or not talking. But all in the same room, all in the same place, gathering together in a way they weren't allowed to do before.

Draw back farther. We are standing in the eaves.

Say hi if you see us.

Silence equals death, we'd say. And underneath that would be the assumption—the fear—that death equaled silence.

Sometimes you glimpse that horror. Someone gets sick. Someone gets sent to war. Someone takes his own life.

Every day a new funeral. It was such a large part of our existence.

You have no idea how fast things can change. You have no idea how suddenly years can pass and lives can end.

Ignorance is not bliss. Bliss is knowing the full meaning of what you have been given.

We watch you, but we don't intervene. We have already done our part. Just as you are doing your part, whether you know it or not, whether you mean to or not, whether you want to or not.

Choose your actions wisely.

There will come a time—perhaps even by the time you read this—when people will no longer be on Facebook. There will come a time when the stars of *High School Musical* will be sixty. There will come a time when you will have the same inalienable rights as your straightest friend. (Probably before any of the stars of *High School Musical* turns sixty.) There will come a time when the gay prom won't have to be separate. There will come a time when you will be able to listen to any song ever recorded or watch any movie ever made, no matter where you are. There will come a time when you will worry about being forgotten. There will come a time when the gospel will be rewritten.

If you play your cards right, the next generation will be so much different from your own.

On the day that Ryan and Avery get married at a church in South Carolina, they will read for their vows a poem written by Ricky Schiller. When Avery gets to the last line, his best man, Erik Johnson, will have a tear in his eye. Not from loneliness—he will be happily single his whole life—but from the perfection of the moment. In the seventh row, Neil Hayden will find himself wondering about his high-school boyfriend, Peter . . . and three months later, he will be walking through a park and Peter's dog will run over to him, and bring her owner along, too.

Amazing, no?

Welcome to the attainable world.

We saw our friends die. But we also see our friends

live. So many of them live, and we often toast their long and full lives. They carry us on.

There is the sudden. There is the eventual.
  And in between, there is the living.

We do not start as dust. We do not end as dust. We make more than dust.
  That's all we ask of you: Make more than dust.

HAPPILY EVER AFTER

·

BY ERIC SHANOWER

HAPPILY EVER AFTER

by **ERIC SHANOWER**

MY BEST FRIEND, MARK, AND I WOULD GO DOWN TO THE CREEK AFTER SCHOOL AND MAKE OUT FOR--I DON'T KNOW--*HOURS* MAYBE.

THE TIME ALWAYS SEEMED TOO SHORT.

THE PREVIOUS YEAR I'D TOLD MY PARENTS I WAS GAY. THEY DIDN'T EXACTLY JUMP UP AND DOWN WITH JOY, BUT THEY DIDN'T HAVE ANY MAJOR PROBLEM WITH IT.

HEY!

I TOLD YOU NOT TO DO THAT!

NO ONE EXCEPT ME KNEW ABOUT MARK. NOT FOR *SURE*, ANYWAY. HIS PARENTS WOULD HAVE GONE *BALLISTIC*.

OKAY, MARK... CAN'T BLAME A GUY FOR TRYING.

NOT THAT I EVER SAW BRUISES, BUT THE FIRST TIME I SAW MARK'S DAD SCREAM AT HIM AND HIS LITTLE BROTHERS WAS THE *LAST* TIME I'D BEEN INSIDE HIS HOUSE.

BUT YOU *KEEP* TRYING AND IT *RUINS* IT!

I'VE SEEN YOU NAKED IN GYM CLASS *PLENTY* OF TIMES. WHAT'S THE DIFF?

I KNEW THINGS WERE MORE DIFFICULT FOR MARK. BUT THAT DIDN'T MEAN I DIDN'T *WISH* THINGS WERE EASIER.

THAT'S *TOTALLY* DIFFERENT, AND YOU KNOW IT!

YEAH, I KNOW-- GRIND INTO EACH OTHER ALL WE WANT WITH OUR PANTS ON, THEN GO HOME TO JERK OFF ALONE. IT'S *CRAZY*!

I BOW BEFORE YOU WITH DEEPEST GRATITUDE, O MASTER. TO THE ONE WHO HAS FOUND THE BOTTLE AND RELEASED ME FROM LONG IMPRISONMENT, I AM BOUND TO GRANT ONE WISH.

UH--

I FOUND THE BOTTLE!

DOES HE SPEAK TRULY, O MASTER?

UH--YES--*MARK* FOUND THE BOTTLE AND *I* LET YOU OUT.

CURIOUS! THERE IS NO PRECEDENT FOR SUCH A CIRCUMSTANCE...

NO MATTER! CENTURIES OF TRADITION CLAMOR AGAINST IT, BUT I CAN CONCEIVE OF NO SATISFACTORY ALTERNATIVE. I SHALL DIVIDE THE WISH IN TWO AND GRANT EACH OF YOU WHAT HE DESIRES.

WE EACH GET A WISH? *REALLY?*

YOU *DOUBT* THE WORD OF GENIE FOUADI-WADI-NASR-RAS-DAROUN-BOUN-ALI-MEHT-MA-HANI-PAL THE PERSPICACIOUS? WHEN A *GENIE* GRANTS A WISH IT COMES TRUE.

THEN I WISH...

FOR MARK AND ME...

TO BE TOTALLY IN LOVE WITH EACH OTHER AND LIVE HAPPILY EVER AFTER!

AS THE DAYS PASSED, MY WISH FOR MARK TO BE IN LOVE WITH ME SEEMED TO BE A FAILURE. HE WOULDN'T TAKE MY PHONE CALLS, WOULDN'T ANSWER EMAIL.

WHEN I WENT OVER TO HIS HOUSE, HIS DAD CALLED ME A LITTLE FAGGOT AND TOLD ME NEVER TO COME BACK.

I STILL FELT THE SAME AS EVER ABOUT MARK--THE WAY I'D FELT SINCE THE FIRST DAY OF SIXTH GRADE, THE DAY I SAID "HI" TO THE BOY WITH THE SHINIEST HAIR I'D EVER SEEN.

I DIDN'T NEED A WISH FOR THAT.

THEN MONTHS STARTED TO PASS. WHENEVER I SAW MARK--ALWAYS AT A DISTANCE--HE WAS EITHER ALONE OR WITH SOME GIRL HANGING ON HIM.

I TOOK SOLACE IN THE REALIZATION THAT IT WAS RARELY THE SAME GIRL TWICE.

A YEAR PASSED BY. THEN ANOTHER. I TRIED TO CONCENTRATE ON OTHER THINGS, TO FORGET MARK AND THE WISHES AND HOW MISERABLE I WAS.

BUT THIS WAS NO WAY TO LIVE "HAPPILY EVER AFTER."

IN SENIOR YEAR I WAS ACCEPTED BY A UNIVERSITY FAR FROM HOME. I HEARD THAT MARK WAS GOING TO A COLLEGE FAR AWAY TOO.

IT WAS A RELIEF TO KNOW I WOULDN'T BE CATCHING ANY MORE GLIMPSES OF HIM FLEEING INTO THE DISTANCE, BUT IT KIND OF HURT TOO.

THE FIRST SEMESTER AT UNIVERSITY WAS TOUGH. BUT THAT HELPED TAKE MY MIND OFF MARK.

MY LIFE AS A DOG

·

BY RON KOERTGE

When Noah's a dog, the best part is remembering things from his other life. So he's like a human in a dog's body. The smartest dog in the galaxy. It's the best of both worlds in a way. He's fearless about taking a canine crap, for instance, but inhibited and pretty much chronically constipated as a human. But he's aware of his fearlessness, so he gets to relish it.

Once he was staying with these two guys, both named Chip. They found him running loose, checked for a collar and tags, and then took him home. Chip #1 works as a clothes salesman and worries about his looks. Chip #2 is rough-and-tumble, and the tattoo across his shoulders says, LIFE IS A DUST-STREWN PLAIN. Guess who stays out all night and guess who stays home tapping his gold-and-amethyst ring on the coffee cup and staring at the clock? Number 2 comes in looking pleased with himself after an evening with a few anti-friends. He's glad to see Noah. Glad to get down on one knee. He sports one of those beards of depravity, like Peter O'Toole in *Becket*. To Noah, he smells like he's been eating chicken in a jeep and smoking opium. "How are you, boy? Are you a good boy?" He slaps him on the muzzle and Noah pretends to bite at his hand, which circles like one of LAPD's sky pigs over West Hollywood.

Number 1 says, "Leave that dog alone, and tell me what you value in our relationship."

Number 2 replies, "The way you can microwave Tater Tots?"

"Get out!"

But that's code, and Noah knows what for. He pads over to his bowl, eats, then lies down. Number 1 uses the hurt look Noah has seen him practice in the mirror. After which he kneels beside him and croons, "You love me, don't you, boy?" Sure. Unconditional love for thirty or forty bucks a month. Or whatever dog food costs these days. Noah wouldn't know. His parents, Martin and Aimee, never let him have a dog. Not when he was little, certainly not now when he's twenty (or almost three in dog years). A couple of weeks ago, Noah trotted into a Safeway Market, took a can of Mighty Dog off the shelf, and carried it to a checkout line in his mouth. He was cute as hell. People fell all over themselves trying to pay for it.

INT. A HOSPITAL ROOM: DAY

AIMEE

He was hit by a car. The driver never stopped. The doctor says he's lucky to be alive.

MARTIN

Did anybody see anything? Aimee? Were there witnesses?

AIMEE

Noah was conscious when the ambulance got there. He said something about a blue van.

MARTIN

I'll make some calls. Why doesn't he say anything?

AIMEE

He goes in and out of consciousness.
The doctor says that can happen.

MARTIN

He's barking. Does the doctor say
that can happen?

AIMEE

Martin, please sit down.

MARTIN

And do what—wait? You know I'm
not good at waiting. Where are his
car keys? Where was he, anyway, at
one of those movies of his?

AIMEE

The police said something about West
Hollywood.

MARTIN

West Hollywood? What was he doing
in West Hollywood?

Sometimes Noah goes home with girls. Single gals. Pretty little things. Slender kiosks hung with trinkets. He waits outside a supermarket. The night like velour. "Whose little dog are you?" asks the fairy-tale voice.

A caress. A hand on his forehead like the night nurse checking for fever. He trots toward the parking lot. She says, "Go back, doggie. You can't come home with me."

But he can and does. Some return to the market and ask every insomniac and night-shift worker if they own the dog sitting outside. No? No? No? Are you sure?

Others just let him right into their durable little economy cars. "Can I trust you?" they all ask because he is riding beside a week's worth of groceries: cottage cheese, canned pineapple, glacier water, a thousand yogurts.

He shows his bright, blameless eyes. And his tongue, innocent as the red carpet in the Garden of Eden. They all pet him and say, "You're a good boy, aren't you? Aren't you a good boy?"

They're happy for a while. There's always a rug in the suburbs of the bed. There's always walking and flirting. They go places they used to avoid because he makes them less fearful. At home, they talk on the phone in their underwear while he noses around the hamper. The smells are intoxicating! (A certain Denise did not have days-of-the-week underwear but a kind of Adjective Panty: Solitude, Lassitude, Interlude, Gratitude, Semi-Nude, Quaalude, Platitude.)

They all give him a name and their friends ask about him. On weekends they cry sometimes, undo the latch of their secrets, and out they come. And they're everybody's.

Sometimes, an inamorata objects to Noah's presence and plays the Either-That-Dog-Goes-or-I-Go game. At that point, he runs away.

Usually, though, his leaving starts with candy. Fine. He doesn't want to drift through their lives anymore. Where's somebody who will wrestle with him and throw a big, heavy stick? More candy, a little ice cream. And, right on cue, he pukes.

A few hit him, but mostly they say, "Oh doggie. No." Demoted from Boomer or Duke or Spenser to the generic. Then it's right into the car. Right back to that market.

Once in a while, he's taken a long way. For Noah, the air everywhere is alive and humming. Even in the desert below Twentynine Palms. None of them ever wants to see him again. He was a nice dog, but he couldn't be trusted. "Get out!"

Easy as pie. He trots along the side of the road. Cars swing wide to avoid him. Wolves are running in his blood. He laughs out loud. Pretty soon somebody slows, stops, puts on their hazard lights. He trots right up, sits, and offers to shake hands. Which just about stops their hearts.

INT. A HOSPITAL ROOM: DAY

MARTIN
Why does he twitch like that?

DOCTOR
He's dreaming. Or it's like dreaming.

MARTIN
Well, he looks like a damn cocker
spaniel.

DOCTOR
When he was admitted, he had fleas.

MARTIN

I beg your pardon?

DOCTOR

Fleas. So we were wondering—

MARTIN

My house is spotless. My wife sees to
that.

DOCTOR

We were wondering if your son
worked with animals.

MARTIN

He goes to UCLA. He's in film
school. I've met a few of his friends
and I wouldn't be surprised if they
were infected.

Breakfast with Noah's owners. Or rather his parents.
He can't imagine Aimee and Martin having sex. It's not
unimaginable; he just can't imagine it. Or kissing even.
As Martin leaves to sit behind his big desk at the bank,

Noah's seen them pretend to kiss, but it's brusque and perfunctory. What the shoe does to the doormat on a sunny day.

Sometimes Robbie and Noah suck on a cough drop and pass it back and forth until it's gone, and it's a thousand times more passionate.

His father orders the newspaper around. He opens it like a sail. Closes it like a door. Folds it like a map. He hoards it, his big hand on the pieces not in front of his face.

He asks, "Noah, what's on your agenda today?"

"I've got an exam."

"In what?"

"History of film."

"Well, when that gets you nowhere, just let me know. I make one call and you've got a desk and a client list." He lifts his cup of coffee, scowls at it. "Noah, get me the Sweet'n Low."

Noah's mother immediately stands up.

"No," his father says. "I want Noah to do it."

As he fetches, Noah wonders what he could say that might make his father happy.

Medical school this morning, Dad, and law school this afternoon, dinner with you and Mom tonight. Jo Ann's coming. Remember when you had her DNA checked and she turned out to be related to God?

No wonder he likes being a dog. The transformation is easy. None of that horror-movie stuff with the taut skin, the crackling ligaments, and the screaming in pain. He's not Lon Chaney in *The Wolfman*, ruining a perfectly good suit every month. He just goes to sleep human and wakes up canine. He loves the feeling. He's not as comfortable in his Noah body. The Homo sapiens one. A dog body is enthusiastic, not fretting and anxious, like the other one.

When he first opens his eyes, he doesn't know which he is, and then seconds later he does. Mostly it's the smells and the way they petition him. The funk and flavor of blood, a festival of rat shit in the walls, the whole secret society of the soiled and redolent.

When he's a human, Noah thinks all the time. He looks at the books he bought. Those books—*Boy Meets Boy, When I Knew, That's Mr. Faggot to You.* They're a comfort in a way, but he knows who he is. That's not the problem. It's the ones who don't know. And what they'd think and say and do if they found out.

What was he going to do with those books, anyway?

Stack them on his father's desk and hope he gets the hint? He might as well dig a hole and bury them in the backyard.

Except he'd never dig a hole where he wasn't supposed to. He's too well trained. Just like he wouldn't pee on the rug. He's housebroken, too. In every sense of the word.

Noah looks around Robbie's apartment. He likes it here. He feels comfortable, more like himself—whoever that is. Not that he's not anxious. He's always anxious.

He says, "I told my mother I was going to the gym."

Robbie puts down the plate he's been drying. "Well, if my name was Jim, that would barely be a lie. What do homophones count on your list of punishable offenses? And speaking of homophones, those are available from AT&T if you're out of the closet, so you aren't eligible."

Noah could live in an apartment like this. Nice things, a notch or two above IKEA. Not here, though. In a place of his own.

"I'm going to tell them," he says.

"Your mother knows, anyway. Mothers always know."

Noah points to the TV screen. It's *CSI Miami*, with all of its glamour and dissection. "What's wrong with David Caruso's neck?"

Robbie angles his neck, too. "When he looks sort of sideways like that, he's about to discover something everybody else on the forensics team has missed. Like that spleen pulsing in the gutter."

"Why do you watch this crap?"

"Everybody's got a guilty pleasure, Noah. This is mine. Unless you'd rather play Bambi Goes to the Salt Lick."

"Don't talk that way."

"Somebody has to."

If Noah were a dog, he could do anything he wanted anytime he wanted. Dogs don't have inhibitions.

Noah apologizes. "I'm sorry I'm so tentative."

"That's all right. You're a kid."

"I'm not either!"

"You go to school. You live with your parents. That adds up to kid for me." Robbie crosses from the kitchen and sits beside Noah. "I found something on the net for you the other day. A fact-ette. In the

Bible, in Ezekiel, it's very clear that the sin of Sodom wasn't homosexuality. It was inhospitality toward travelers from the desert."

Noah turns so he can see Robbie, look right into his eyes. "You always knew you were gay."

"Always."

"And it didn't bother you?"

"Why should it bother me? Even as I child I was hospitable toward travelers from the desert. I let them park their camels in my yard."

"Is that true, that thing from Ezekiel?"

"That's what it said right on my computer screen. Do you want some lunch?"

"Sure. We could go out. You're always fixing things. I should pay or bring groceries or something."

Robbie pats Noah's shoulder briskly. "Not necessary. You just sit here and watch David Caruso find the smoking mortar shell casing in the delphiniums, and I'll throw a few things together."

On the screen, a policeman runs with his K-9 companion. Noah is a pretty good runner, but nothing like when he changes. As a dog he's drunk with running, that long aria of the body at its best. Thoughtless in the best sense of the word.

He watches Robbie cook—sees his strong arms, admires his shaved head and on his neck the tattoo that dives into his T-shirt and doesn't stop until it reaches his left nipple.

"When you were little," Robbie asks, "did you spell out dirty words in your alphabet soup?"

"Are you kidding? My parents would have caught me."

"Parents?"

"All right, my mother. Didn't your mother keep an eye on you?"

"When I was little, we lived in New York. There are no soup censors in New York. But there was this little pocket park with a sandbox and swings and a slide right across the street from our building, and she'd send me over there alone."

Noah gets to his feet, almost propelled by the news. "Wow."

There's a kind of breakfast bar with two stools that separates the kitchen from the dining room. Noah looks at Robbie from his side. Robbie's holding a stalk of celery like a baton. He could be somebody from a children's book, the conductor of an orchestra of vegetables. Professor Von Garden.

"I thought it was cool, too," Robbie says. "There were always other kids with their moms or their nannies. I was never there alone. For another thing, my mother was watching me through her binoculars. If anything looked even the least bit fishy she would've dialed nine-one-one."

"What did she do all day? Why didn't she come downstairs to the playground with you?"

"She didn't like the sun."

"Was she a vampire?"

"Actually she was a corsetiere."

Noah leans on the counter so he can see all the way to Robbie's feet, bare in a pair of dilapidated moccasins. "Is a corsetiere what I think it is?"

Robbie nods. "She made corsets, and not just for women, either. Drag queens came by, B & D people, or just guys who liked tight things under their suits. She was discreet and egalitarian."

"I know what you're going to say next. That I'm wearing one already, the Closeted Queer model."

"If you say so." He turns to Noah with a smile and points to a large bowl of salad. "What kind of dressing do you want on this?"

INT. HOSPITAL: DAY

ROBBIE

Don't bullshit me. You weren't hit by
any van. Somebody beat you up.

NOAH

Shut up.

ROBBIE

Where?

NOAH

Just . . . off Santa Monica Boulevard.
Where I'd parked the car.

ROBBIE

So you lied to the cops.

NOAH

They're not going to catch the guys.
What's the point of getting into all
that?

ROBBIE

All what?

NOAH

All that "What were you doing there at two A.M.?"

ROBBIE

The police don't care what time it was.

NOAH

I wasn't talking about the police.

ROBBIE

Ah, the Aimee & Martin show.

NOAH

It's not a show. It's real.

ROBBIE

It's drama, Noah. Everything's drama to you. How many screenplays have you shown me? All you care about is the story arc. Well, do this one justice and give it a satisfying conclusion.

NOAH

But if the cops know, everybody will know.

ROBBIE

Everybody doesn't care if you're gay or not.

NOAH

My parents, then.

ROBBIE

You mean your dad.

NOAH

He treats me like a dog, I swear to god. Sit up, roll over, heel. I should just run away.

ROBBIE

Except a dog that runs away is a lost dog. Tail between his legs, flea-bitten and pathetic.

NOAH

So what should I do? I can't bite
him. You know what they do with
biters, don't you? They put them
down.

ROBBIE

You don't have to bite him. Just lose
the collar and leash.

NOAH

It's hard.

ROBBIE

Nobody said it wasn't. But you're not
a stray dog or a lone wolf. You've got
me.

NOAH

I wasn't doing anything that night.
Just playing pool and, you know,
dancing a little and being someplace
where everybody was like me.

ROBBIE

The bars are fun. We should go.
Shoot some stick. Dance a little. Get
all sweaty and take off our shirts.

NOAH

Kiss me, okay?

ROBBIE

Here in front of Doctor God and
everybody?

NOAH

Absolutely!

Everybody calls it Bark Park, and Noah loves it. He gets
to come here whenever he wants—no ride in the car,
no waiting at the corner, no commands, no lord and
master to tell him, "Go!" Especially no master.

He works his way through the bushes at the deep
end of the park, then bursts onto the scene. There are so
many dogs, so many owners, so much tumult, so many
high spirits that nobody notices him on his own. Free,
unshackled, uncurbed, unsane, un-everything.

He breaks into a trot, then races a malamute named Soldier, nips playfully at Sue the collie, vaults over Puppy Longstocking. Half-drunk on the scent of all things wonderful, he picks up a stick and gets into a tug-of-war with Lewis, a big, yellow Lab. They brace and growl, their teeth glow in the dusk. They drop the stick and sprint recklessly. Noah's body is beautiful and perfect. It will do anything he wants. This freedom is a passport to everything.

Lights come on in the buildings across the way. Owners check watches and answer phones. Whistles of every kind—sharp and dark, soft and light. Commands gentle or harsh but always commands. Hand to the collar again. Click of the lead, the choker, the harness, the tether, the rope. The pat on the head. The heel.

Except for Noah, panting and alive, exhausted and ready for more. Standing there on his own four feet.

INT. HOSPITAL: DAY

MARTIN
The police are still looking for that
blue van. I made some calls. I know
people.

NOAH

They won't find it, because it wasn't
a van. It was just two guys who beat
me up because they thought I was
gay.

AIMEE

Oh, my god.

MARTIN

Didn't you tell them?

NOAH

They weren't in the mood for expla-
nations, Dad. And, anyway, they
were right. I am gay.

MARTIN

This is the medication talking.

NOAH

I should have told you before. A long
time ago.

MARTIN

You were engaged to Jo Ann.

NOAH

That's what you told people. Jo Ann
and I got to be friends. We still are,
actually. I only went out with women
because you wanted me to.

MARTIN

This is going to destroy your mother.
After all we've done for you.

NOAH

Actually, you treated me like a dog.
And I let you, all for a rug by the fire
and a biscuit. But not anymore, Dad.
Not anymore.

MARTIN *(as he exits)*

I'm not listening to this.

AIMEE

I'd better go take care of your father.

He'll drink too much coffee. *(kissing him)* I'll see you tomorrow.

INT. HOSPITAL: DAY

NOAH *(zipping up a small carry on)*
This looks like everything.

AIMEE
Your father couldn't come.

NOAH
I'm stunned.

AIMEE
He loves you, he does.

At a knock on the door, they both turn. A POLICE-MAN enters.

POLICEMAN
You wanted to talk to me?

NOAH

I, uh, wasn't exactly candid when I
told you about what happened to me.

POLICEMAN

And you want to be candid now.

NOAH

There wasn't any van. I got beat up.
It was a gay bashing. I'm gay.

POLICEMAN

Description?

NOAH

White guys. High-school kids, probably. Jeans and hoodies. They work at
McDonald's or one of those fast food
places.

POLICEMAN

How do you know that?

NOAH

They smelled like grease and cheap
meat. I know what I'm talking about.
I have a highly developed sense of
smell.

END

TREV

·

BY JACQUELINE WOODSON

The first dream came when I was five years old. Already, only in kindergarten, I was a head taller than the other students and sharing shoes with my ten-year-old brother. When my teacher first saw me, she stuttered, looking from me to my information in her book—*Girl*, it must have said. Or *Female*. Or *She*.

But kindergarten didn't last. Kindergarten was dangerous. On the first day a girl in a pink dress, her hair tied with too many ribbons, stopped me at the bathroom door. *You are so not coming in here*, she said, glaring at my khaki pants, my blue-striped button-down shirt, my new cowboy boots. We were sent to the bathroom in partners, and my partner, a girl named Rose who held my hand with her sweaty own as we walked down the hallway, let go of my hand quickly when the pink child spoke. Then Rose moved to stand beside the girl, her hand fluttering gently up to the ribbons.

When I pushed past the pink girl, I pushed her

down. When she was down, I didn't know that I hated her for her too many ribbons, for every pink dress she'd ever worn and stepped out proudly in, for her hand blocking my entrance, for the way she said *You are* so *not . . .* Because I *was*. I *was* going into that bathroom. I *was* going to walk where I wanted. I *was* going to kick her until someone pulled me off.

I hated her because I *am*.

Kindergarten was dangerous because I didn't know the rules. And because of this, I was given another year at home to learn them, to understand. Another year away from girls in pink dresses saying how and when.

And now, here I was, a first grader with a note from my mother. *Please excuse my daughter's lateness to her first day. The day started out wrong.* But the day had begun as any other day—my brother's rage hot in the room. *You must be high if you think I'm walking to school with her.* My mother's frustration. *Wear the dress, Trev, it's your first day.* And me, all of six and already rooted. *Hell no, Ma.*

Our family is like that.

All summer long my brother had managed to avoid me—turning corners when he saw me coming, heading upstairs if he saw me heading down, walking out the back door as I entered the front, tossing the remote on the couch and leaving the TV room when I came into it. . . . Always the summer had been coming to this moment—when he entered fourth grade and I entered first. The school-bus ride, the walking me down the hall and to my class, the handing me off to my teacher, his queer little sister who screamed when her mother suggested a cornflower blue dress—that's what she'd called it, *cornflower*—as if the color or the flower made any sense. Corn. Flower. Cornflower blue. *What the hell is wrong with you?* my mother said, and even though she wasn't supposed to, she lit a cigarette in front of us and took a deep drag of it before tossing the dress on the couch.

What the hell is wrong with you? I didn't move. Just folded my arms and stared at her. There was a knife in my pocket. A penknife my friend Alex had given me. Red handled and sharpened all summer long on the curb outside our house. The blade was as thin as a razor. I fingered the handle—cool and smooth.

Then you *figure out what the hell you're wearing*, my mother said.

And I did. So here I was, standing in front of this pretty new teacher, the scent of my father's Domme hair products wafting from my curls, the top button left just so, and my skin showing through it—caramel, golden, nut brown, honey, depending on who was looking and what mood they were in. . . .

But it was not the note my mother wrote that threw her—I know this now. It was the jeans and the button-down shirt and the hair, cut short over my ears and the tight curls just on top. *Daughter?* her eyes said. But she was young and pretty and it was her first year teaching, so her lips trembled up into a smile.

Trev, I said. *Trev Louis Johnson.*

Six years before, on a cloudy day in June—*too cold for June*, my mother said—I was born Trevana Louise Johnson. For my father, Trevor. For my mother, Dana. His father was Trevor, too. Her grandmother Dane Alise. The line goes back and back until old people can't remember where it started. I was born a combination of grandmothers and grandfathers and blood and vowels mixing until I came into this world—a new combination of black and white, of my mother's dark skin and my father's pale. *Dark-eyed and already mad about something*, my mother said.

I knew I wasn't right.

Have a seat right here, Trev, my teacher said. And

in the way of great first-grade teachers everywhere, she folded herself around this daughter-boy that was me.

That night, in the dream, I unzipped my six-year-old self and stepped out—free.

Breathe, my mother said. *Just breathe.*

That summer before, as my brother ran away from me, I had learned to breathe—first with my mother and when that wasn't enough, then with Dr. K, who had me draw pictures and choose clothes from wooden crates and play pretend with pale bendable dolls. Dr. K, with her patient *Do you want to talk about it?*, to which the answer was always *No*, but somehow the words made their way into the room. *I'm wrong down there.* All summer long *I'm wrong down there*, until Dr. K with her limber dolls and button-down dress-up shirts and mirrors and words showed me that other world, the world inside the world.

Each night thereafter, I closed my eyes, took deep breaths until in that place between sleep and wake, I unzipped this world I wore.

And now, a year since my first day as a kindergartner, I was allowed back again—a first grader—taller, breathing, a knife in my pocket as sharp as my brother's rage. But it was all different. My father—the Trev part of me—had left in late July, a small suitcase packed, a kiss on each of our foreheads, my mother turning away from the window in tears. My father's world inside his world was crumbling. He had dreamed me pink and girlie. He had dreamed princess parties and sweet six-teens, a wedding dance before handing me off to his new and beloved son-in-law. He'd said this: *She's killing me. I'm a man and my little girl is killing me.* But in my world inside my world, I knew he wasn't talking about me, because I wasn't his little girl. I was Trev. And Trev was *not* a girl.

Dr. K had sat them down, slowly re-explained me.

But you can fix that, can't you? my father had asked. *Can't someone fix her?*

Trev is Trev, Dr. K had said. *Let him be so.*

And my father pressed his face into his hands and cried.

I am not a little girl.

You're a fuckin' freak! my brother had screamed. And for days our house was filled with a silence so sharp at its edges, so cold. For days our house was as cold and fragile as glass.

You chased him away, my brother said, but my mother shook her head.

Your father was already halfway gone.

In first grade, my teacher was Ms. Riley. Call me *Ms. R*, she said, or *Ms. Riley or Cara, if you like.*

Cara? we said, our eyebrows knitting up, our hands going over our mouths. Cara was too human, too right here and now. Teachers weren't Cara.

Cara, she said. *It was my grandmother's name.*

Then we spent time talking about where our names came from, whether or not we liked them, what we'd change them to. And when I told the history of my name, the class listened, some even smiled at me.

Dane had come before me. She was my mother's great-aunt, tall and cigar smoking and handsome. She laughed with her head thrown back and wore her hair cut low. In the pictures, Dane looks directly into the camera as though she's daring something to come closer. *It's like she's wearing a shield, right?* I asked my brother one night when he was still a friend of mine. But he couldn't see it. Couldn't see that Dane was a true-blue superhero.

Maybe I'll be a superhero, too.

Some nights, I dreamed I was flying above the world, my cape trailing out behind me, silver-gray and shining in the moonlight. I dreamed I looked down and saw others like me and I called to them and they flew up and joined me, and together we circled the earth all night long. And the world was safe. And we were safe.

What happened to Dane? I ask my mother, staring at the picture of her for the hundred-thousandth time.

She cut a man, my mother says. *And they took her away. And when she got out, she never came home again.* Mama looks at the picture and smiles. *I like to think she found a friendlier place somewhere. She had a hard time in our town. But she handled it. She was something else, that Dane.*

Why'd she cut that man?

He probably made her mad. Said something he didn't have a right to be saying to her.

In school sometimes, I touch the knife in my pocket, feel the smooth handle, think about the sharp edge of the blade. One day my mother will find it and lose her mind. Smack me or light up a cigarette or sit down and cry.

Is that thing your sister or brother or whatever it is? the older kids ask my brother sometimes.

Hell no, he says, flicking his eyes away from me, out into the schoolyard, over the other kids who walk the world all lost or safe inside their skin.

On the second day of school, the day that was my first, I walked with a new partner, Raymond, down the hall to the boys' bathroom. When I stepped inside and closed the stall door, I smiled. I was home.

Each night, when my mother kisses my cheek, she pulls the covers up to my ears and whispers, *I wish on eyelashes and birthday candles, tomorrow you'll be my sugar and spice and everything nice.* Then, I turn onto my back, close my eyes, and breathe deeply until the dream is there.

And in the dream, I am a boy, truly, everywhere. In the dream, no one looks twice at me. No one laughs. No little girl screams, no brother turns away. In the dream, there is one world, the right one, and superhero me has swooped down.

And saved it from mortal destruction.

MY VIRTUAL WORLD

·

BY FRANCESCA LIA BLOCK

i don't have a body here. it is a relief not to have a body. i am just a face. i float around on the music of my choice. i have a lot of friends. they are disembodied, too. we don't argue. we don't hear each other's voices, only the songs we love. we don't touch but it's all right. our words touch. it's easier to live in this world we've created, everyone beautiful in their pics, all the pain contained in poetry and drawings and photographs. it's easier to love this way. you

feel seen. you

feel

heard.

but you're not really.

dear ms. r. e.

thanks for the add. i really like your pictures and what you wrote about in your blog. you look/sound sad/happy at the same time.

yours,
blue boy

dear blue boy

thank you! i like your pictures, too. you look so hot, especially that one in the hat with the shadows on your face and the cigarette hanging from your lip. your artwork is beautiful. i love those dark paintings of the mermaids and centaurs. tell me more about them.

ms. r. e.

i stare at my wrists. they have these white seams along them. sometimes i hide them under sleeves and jewelry. sometimes i want you all to see them. i want you to worry about me, to be impressed, a little afraid. i want you to hold them to your lips and see if you can feel the marks, like braille, and if you can read the story they write.

dear ms. r. e.

i did those paintings when i was in rehab last year. it really helped me. i was having a hard time. they were about not feeling integrated in my body. how are you doing? your blog sounded really sad today. what story do your scars tell?

bb

hi blue

about two years ago i started cutting myself. it was the weirdest thing. i felt so powerful. i don't admit this to most people but it was almost beautiful. the way the blood beaded on my skin and that feeling of being close to death but in control of how close. which is not how it is when your dad dies of cancer. that is pure out of control.

after my dad died i got together with this guy and it helped at first but after a while it got really crazy. i think i scared him. i'd write to him all the time and give him things and want to talk about my feelings. he broke up with me and i wanted to take the cutting further. now i'm in therapy with a really good therapist and it is helping.

yesterday the guy called me and wanted to get together. that kind of set me off.

i think i said too much. sorry. i always say too much.

i'm sorry you had a hard time last year. you can tell me about it if you want to. i hope things are much better.

today the weather can't decide what it is doing. there was sun trying to break through the clouds but now the darkness hangs overhead waiting to turn into rain.

rebecca

dear rebecca

thank you for sharing that with me. you didn't say too much. i am glad you trusted me. but may i ask you why you trust me?

b (garret)

garret

i trust you because of your eyes in the pictures. they are wide open and very kind. i
trust you because you like old cat stevens
songs and are not afraid to post them.
also, anyone who loves krishna das is cool.
he opens my heart and makes me cry. but
mostly, it's your artwork. there is so much
pain in it but also beauty.

my therapist told me that i should wait and
see if people are deserving of my trust but
i don't always do that.

rebecca

why aren't you here? what did i do to
frighten you away? i used to think this
capacity to love was going to draw you
to me. i had no idea it would scare you
so much. i stare at the untouched skin on
my wrists. it is so white and smooth still.

it reminds me of a canvas waiting for its paint.

rebecca

i am worried about you. i hope you are not hurting yourself.

thank you for your kind words about me. i am feeling a little blue today. staying at home with my cats. they keep walking across the keyboard and sending strange messages so don't be shocked if you get one that seems to be from me but is actually written by a feline.

take care. really.

g.

p.s.

i am attaching a self-portrait i made. it is a little dark, well a lot dark actually, so i didn't post it in case my mom saw it, because she has a myspace account now. my art therapist encouraged me to make art instead of drinking too much. do you feel you could keep from cutting yourself by writing more? i don't mean to interfere but you are on my mind.

blue boy

i'm doing o.k. thanks. i'm sad about that boy i like. i don't know why i still like him. i have so much love inside of me and i don't think boys can handle it. you seem different.

you look like you are in so much pain in that painting. have you ever thought about the word pain in painting? it is amazing, though, how you can take pain and make it into something so beautiful. the way your hands are tearing your chest open so tenderly and the color of your heart . . .

what are your cats' names?

bec

hi

i am sitting here with my cats climbing all over me. their names are piggy and sas-safras. i love them very much. i understand how you feel with all that love to give. it is a beautiful thing. tonight i wish i could give you a hug and make you feel better.

i'm sending you a drawing i did of you from one of your photos.

xo garret

blue

i love that picture! thank you so much! i don't really like how i look but that picture is how i want to look, how i feel inside.

can i ask you something? why do you seem to understand me so well? you aren't like any boy i have ever met. do you want to meet in person sometime? i think i have a myspace crush on you.

r.

this is weird to write.

i am not like any boy you ever met because i was not born a boy. i should have told you this right away. i'm attaching a picture of myself before. if you are freaked out and don't want to contact me again, i understand. you said you trusted me and i guess it was not very trustworthy of me not to let you know right away.

g.

p.s. i know one thing about myself and that is that i am a very accurate artist and that picture i made looks just like you in the photos. you are beautiful.

rebecca

i hope i didn't freak you out. i don't mean to bug you but i'm a big worrier and i think i might have upset you and that's why you haven't written back. i'm sorry if i upset you.

garret blue

dear garret

i was really surprised by your message. but i understand. i'm sorry i didn't write back immediately but i had to process everything for a couple of days. i just kept staring at that picture of you as mandy over and over again. you looked like you then, too. i am not as shocked as you think.

it's funny because i always wished i could like girls. i kind of idealized lesbians in some way. but i've never even kissed a girl. which is unusual, i think, at least among my friends, who are almost all basically straight.

this may sound like a too personal question but i'm wondering if you think that a straight girl involved with a boy who was born a girl is really a lesbian? i don't mind being a lesbian but i'm not sure that would feel exactly accurate. i have other questions i would like to ask you but i am

a little shy and don't want to make you
uncomfortable.

x

hi rebecca

*thank you! i feel so relieved. i know that
you are not queer but i wondered if maybe
there is some strain of queer blood in you?
i hope that doesn't offend you. you can ask
me any questions you like. it might help
you to look at my pics again, especially the
one in the white briefs.*

tranny boy g.

dear garret

i think that i would rather meet you in
person and ask you my questions then.

except that i do wonder what it was like for you when you were little? when did you know that you weren't comfortable being a girl? did your rehab have to do with all of this?

i also saw that picture you were talking about again. wow you are hot.

does this mean i am now a lesbian?

x

mist r. e.

dear mystery not misery

maybe? do you care?

i never felt like a girl. i always wanted to wear boys' clothes and play with toys that boys usually play with. my body felt strange, like it belonged to somebody else. when i was a teenager i tried to stop eating so that i wouldn't develop or bleed. at twenty-one i started hormone therapy and surgery. it helped but there is a lot of shame i still feel, which is probably why i drank so much, in addition to the fact that i have alcoholism in my genetics. i'm afraid to get too close to anyone because i think they will think there is something really wrong with me for doing what i did to my body.

does this answer your questions?

dear g.

why do you feel shame? there is nothing shameful about who you are. you are a beautiful person. in some cultures, you would be revered as a representative of both sexes. i imagine you are the perfect lover because you are a man who can feel a woman in a true way.

you asked if i care if i'm a lesbian.
no.

last night i got into a fight with my ex-
boyfriend and i wanted to cut myself so
badly but instead i wrote about my feelings. most of it wasn't very good but i
wrote something about you that i think
iś o.k.

i thought about what you have done to
your body and how it is the same but different from what i have done to my body.
it is different if you can still love the little
girl who you were while honoring the man
you have always been and have become.
you were cutting to make yourself whole
and i was cutting to tear myself apart. now
i don't want to do that anymore. i want to
cut with words instead of a knife. i want to
tell you the rest of my story.
i would like to meet you for coffee or tea
or whatever. i have some more things i
would like to share with you about my life

and what my dad did to me and why i cut myself. i know i can trust you.

thank you for being my friend.

love

Sometimes you see them out walking around the city. It's hard to figure them out at first. He looks like a very thin gay man with close-cropped white-blond hair. She looks like a slightly goth young woman, not much more than a teenager. Her hair is straight and black and falls into her eyes, partially covering her face. She wears black lace dresses over tattered leggings and lace-up boots. Sometimes a beaded cashmere vintage cardigan or a fake-fur jacket. They are almost the same height. To bulk up his narrow shoulders, he wears a white T-shirt, a gray hooded sweatshirt and a black leather jacket. He has on Levi's and the same boots that she has. They hold hands a bit tentatively.

Sometimes people stare at them, wondering

what their story is. If you look closely enough you can see it written on his chest and along her wrists, but they're not going to show you because you are only a pair of eyes that can't really see them, a pair of ears that won't really hear.

They will buy groceries and go quietly back to their apartment with the cats and the claw-foot bathtub. They will make tofu and rice and vegetables for dinner. They will put on music intended to make them cry. They won't be ghosts, little postage-stamp-sized faces floating disembodied on your computer screen. They will be there, in the scarred flesh. And they will tell each other.

A DARK RED LOVE KNOT

·

BY MARGO LANAGAN

The road was a ribbon of moonlight,
over the purple moor,
And the highwayman came riding—
Riding—riding—
The highwayman came riding,
up to the old inn-door.

—Alfred Noyes, *"The Highwayman"*

It was one of those wild nights. Ghost-horses rode up every little while. It was weather for unsettlement, not quite decided to rain, the wind not sure which direction it wanted to prevail from, so trying this way and that way, this strength and that. Even as I came around from the stables I was saying to myself, *Get you back to your straw, Tom. It's cold out and you have only just managed to warm what bed you have.*

The yard was empty. Curse your ears, Tom Coyne, your ears full of horses. But then the wind wafted out the tip of a horse's tail, a little net or veil across some of the moon-shined cobbles of the inn-yard, closer to the house than any horse ever was brought. The man's voice was soft, but it carried on a purpose-shaped gust of wind: "I'm after a prize tonight."

I knew what was up in an instant. I pressed my back to the ivy, and put my ear very carefully to the corner that I might hear without being seen, without him seeing that I saw him.

No more words came, only his secreting voice, and then hers, higher, Miss Black-Eyes', hushed with excitement. Oh, she was not the good girl she painted herself as, that one, chatting with gentlemen out the window of her father's inn.

The ivy waved across my face at the corner, but I got a good look at him. Oh, he was worth seeing, too, standing in his stirrups and the velvet coat blowing around him, debonairness itself. Look at that hat— almost a lady might wear it, it had such style. And then the lace at his throat, like a flag in the moonlight, like a lady's little signal handkerchief bunched in her fine hand at her window, it blew. It leaped and leaned and fought in the wind, which was all confused, that close to the house.

"Before morning," he said.

"You are so certain?"

He laughed low; it rippled through me like horse-flesh shivering off a summer fly. Oh, that was a fine beast he rode—stolen from nobles, no doubt—and some town boy had groomed it; the tail was trimmed straight as a girl's long hair. It was as if he had set himself up, dress and horse and figure, on purpose just to tease me, with what I was not, or with what I could never have.

A rogue wind brought the next as a gift straight from his mouth to my ear: "If they should come after and harry me, I will hide out the day and come for you by night, this very time tomorrow, and our fortune with me."

"You will be careful, won't you?"

His soft laughter came again, again straight to my ears, as if he were just around the house corner from me and laughing *for* me. "I am always careful."

Jealousy—of him, of her, I hardly knew which—stabbed me in the stomach. I looked again and felt rotten with it, at the sight of his smiling mouth, his teeth as white as the lace, his eyes shining at the edge of his hat brim's shadow, his hips wrapped close in the brown breeches, his thighs and shins in the boots.

"You *will* come?" she said, even softer.

He ceased to laugh. He reached up, his face all sharp and intent. He swept his hat off, and bareheaded, he looked even finer, for the slight touslement of his gentleman's locks, the sudden clarity of his eyes, his high, wide brow smooth and white.

"I will come for you, Bess, though hell should bar the way," he said, thrilling me to my foot-soles as I stood spying there.

She reached for him, but the window was too high; she could only touch his fingertips. What a fine hand the man had, not tender and foppish, but long-fingered and strong, a good horseman's hand, I thought, sensitive but commanding should it need to be. It was a hand to haunt my dreams, to make me miserable, while hers hung white and simple in the air above it, so ineffectual-looking—though I knew she was a capable girl and a hard worker—that I could not see why he would grasp after it so longingly.

"Wait—" she said. I half expected her to climb out the window, all petticoats and bosom. But no, she fiddled with her hair, and she loosed it from the knot she had just put it up in, and it fell, longer than her arm and, when she leaned low, longer than his, too, so that it blotted out his throat lace, and his chest was all velvet lapels and her curls.

He picked up handfuls of the stuff and kissed it, his gaze fixed on her face. And she hung above him reaching, blowing kisses, her breasts almost falling out of her bodice, which I dare say she thought would allure him; these shall be yours when you come, when you bring our fortune.

Then he tore himself away, out of her tresses as if from entrapping tentacles. They followed him some way out across the air on the wind. He rode out of the yard, he collected himself in the roadway, he stood his stamping mare and sat straight and sent back a look—it was not for me but it set my bones burning. Who was common Bess, that she should win herself such a look, from such a creature? My God, see him, would you? All a-glitter out there, hilt and pistol butts and boots and brooched hat, and the gleam of dark red velvet, and his burning eyes. He was like some extra constellation, propped above the black-wooded horizon by his gleaming horse.

A word and he was gone—thu-*thudda*, thu-*thudda*, thu-*thudda*—off into the night. She watched him and

I watched him, and even after I could no more see the movement of him against the forest border she was there and I could hear her watching, love-love-love-love with her soupy girl eyes. Then slowly she lowered her window—she must have waxed it, that it didn't squeak—and I heard her affix the shutters inside, slowly too, and there I was alone at the house corner with ivy waving in my face, and the yard and all the road empty.

I ambled back to the stables; I climbed up into the hayloft. "Wha-zah?" said Gramshaw in his pile, surfacing from his dreams of fat Sarah Plummer.

"I thought I heard a horse," I said flatly. "But it was nothing. Just the wind."

The thought punched me in the heart an hour later, sat me up and made me breathless: Tell Bracken. He will send for the king's men.

I half scrambled out of my straw, then sat back in it. Bracken doesn't like to be woken, not for anything.

But what if the gentleman, the robber, should do as he hoped, and come back before dawn, and out she jumps from the window and goes with him? I should be beaten senseless then, for knowing and not saying.

I lay back, my whole body pounding with my pulse. There, then, I told myself. Should that happen, I knew nothing and saw nothing. Should dawn come and the daughter still be here, I shall tell him then; he'll have plenty of time to summon them from the barracks at Chafton.

I burrowed back into the straw, clear awake as if Gramshaw'd bucketed cold water on me. King's men, king's men, here at Bracken's Inn. White-breeched and black-booted, hardened from the Frannitch wars and spoiling for a fight, spoiling for . . . anything they could get their hands on, I could attest to that.

I allowed myself to remember it, how much it hurt, how wonderful it felt, how there had been no shame, I had drunk so exactly the right amount of ale when that narrow-eyed soldier had caught my eye and tilted his head toward the trees. What was he, lieutenant? Captain? He was captain of me, to be sure, he was major-bloody-general, and I was never so happy to be foot soldier or deck swabber or chamber-pot emptier or boot boy or whatever humiliation he might take it in his head to visit on me.

Anyway, it was Chafton Fair, when anything might happen. They were victorious, weren't they, in

Frannishland? So let us ply them with our meat and ale, and no one has to notice, do they, if they lead some colorless ostler boy into the forest and there get naked with him? Let's not speak of it; let them have as they will. They've been a long time at war with their eyes full of death and dark dealings and cannon smoke.

He had me up and down and around about. I cannot tell you how glorious it was, or how confusing, my God. I could not tell, did he love me or hate me? For one moment he was savage at me behind with his claws in my hips and such oaths, such talk in my ears as I'd never heard uttered, saying what he was doing and what he would do, and what kind of filth was I. Then the next he was winding his hot nakedness all around mine, and drinking long drafts of kisses out of my mouth and saying *Who are you* and *Where have you come from* and *No don't answer. Be a mystery to me, a lovely mystery, my darling.*

And so he remained a mystery to me. My darling. I had not realized until he said it that I had waited, all my awkward miserable life, to be a man's darling, just such a man as this, as had been out in the world and seen things, and wore the uniform of worldliness, and would kiss and force and hurt me just so. And since then I had noticed one or two men in their bearing or the fixity of their gaze or the doubleness of their words as might well call me their darling did I give them any sign of wanting it, but I had never yet the exact right amount of ale in me again, and besides, I was still recovering, I was still hoping. If I ever got a chance at that soldier again, I did not want to have been soiled or spoiled by someone else, some farm boy, or that weaselly parson.

King's men. Out the loft window the stars massed and winked. All down in my gut and loins, everywhere he had touched and used, was lapped by warm blood and excited, remembering. If he came to Bracken's, what would I do? Would he manage to sneak away, come up here, kiss me again, and bite me? Of course he would not, but just the thought, just the sight of his narrow eyes recognizing me—a whimper escaped me at the thought. I took a few deep, rough breaths, to assure Gramshaw, should he be awake, that I was not.

Did I sleep then? I hardly know. My mind and blood raced all the night, and as soon as the sky lightened, I got up to watch the house for the master's rising. When I saw lamplight through the slits of his shutters, I went around the back and into the kitchen's light and bustle.

"I need to speak to Mr. Bracken," I said to Cook, who was rolling pastry, one end of the big table.

"Well, come in and shut the door," she says, glaring over at me, "or he won't hear nothing but howling wind."

"I need a word privatelike, and urgent."

"Oh, do you now?" She straightened up, tapped her rolling pin in her hand like a beadle his baton. "Family trouble?" she says confidingly, all her glaringness swept aside by inquisitiveness.

I shook my head. "Just private. And as soon as possible."

She made a careless face. "I will tell him, the moment he can be told anything," she says. "He likes to be left alone i' the mornings."

"I know," said I. "But he will be grateful to know this as early as possible."

She inclined her head, by this acknowledging what I'd said and at the same time dismissing me.

I was well into mucking out when the maid Callie came running, holding her cap on in the wind, its ribbons flying. "Maister wants to see you!" she squeaked.

"I'll be up directly."

She nodded and flew away. I propped my shovel and went to wipe my boots on the grass so I would not foul the house.

They can close out the weather, the rich, can they not? If they want, they can spend all their lives within stone, within quiet, with only the purr of the fire, the rustle of pages of books, the clink of wine decanters. Bracken, I know he gets out and about, but look how he can rest and think and prepare, here in the warmth and upholstery, no? In the tea and the toast and the jug of cream and the dish of conserve.

"What is it, Tom?" he says. I am not yet man enough for him to call me Coyne. "Better make it quick. The mistress'll be along in a minute."

I told him quick and blunt then. I left out all the love stuff, the kisses and the hair and the bosom, the sight of the man's manhood in his tight breeches. I gave him the business straight, the plan I had heard.

He woke as I told him, stopped buttering his toast and hovered there awhile, studying it before putting everything down. Wiped his fingertips on his napkin as he watched me, to disguise their shaking.

"'With our fortune'? He said that?" he asked, cold as cold.

"They were his very words, sir."

Missis bustled in then. She stopped humming when she saw me. Her husband being unusual alert, she came and clutched a scrolly chairback. "Bracken, whatever has happened?"

He held so still, I was afraid he would go off like a bomb in that chair. Except his eyes—like a man looking out the window of a racing carriage, his eyes watched his thoughts rush by.

He stood, as if he was about to come at me and strangle me. "Sit down, my dear," he says, and I realized just in time that he meant his wife. "That will be all, I think, for the moment, Tom. Send Gramshaw to me in my study when you return to your work. Otherwise, no word to anyone. I have a plan and I won't have it spoiled by gossip, you understand?"

"I do, sir," I said, and I left the room, closing the door on the silence inside.

Cook and Callie watched me pass through the kitchen. Out across the yard I hurried, glad to be in the air again, away from that hushed room filling with dangerous feelings. I turned into the stable yard, saw a shovelful of dung drop into a bucket at Cosmos's door.

"Gramshaw!" I called. "Maister has an errand for you!"

News trickled out of the house all day: Bess was confined in her room, the door bolted and a chain and padlock on her window shutters; Gramshaw had ridden off Chafton-ward at a fine clip, on Cosmos himself, with the master's letter—no one knew for whom; Bracken was white with temper and extremely short with everyone; he had taken no breakfast but only paced up and down in his study with the mistress imploring him something, no one was let to hear what.

Callie came and Cook came and Trewissick, who had organized the window lock, and bothered me. "What have you begun?" said Callie, bright eyed, but all her flirting could not get it out of me, nor all Cook's bullying, nor all Trewissick's pretending already to know and clapping me right manly on the shoulder. I did not let a word out, only worked my work, and Gramshaw's too, and waited, heart thumping, for something to happen along the Chafton road.

Gramshaw came back about noon with a sealed note for the master, which he handed in at the kitchen door. Then he came straight for me and delivered me

Cosmos's reins. "Spill it, then, Tom," he said, shrugging off his jacket. "I have just ridden the arse half out of my pants and I wouldn't mind knowing why."

"I promised Bracken not to say a word."

"Even to me? Your stablemate, that has worked beside you all these years? That has just fetched to soldiers—fronted up to king's men!—in regards of some story you've told Bracken? 'Tis the least I deserve, that you tell it me too."

King's men! he had said, as if that were a password, or words of magic—which they almost were, for me, did he but know. They speared me like lightning, and I had to disguise the jolt.

"I promised. I cannot say. It is serious, I tell you."

"They tell me in the kitchen Miss Bess is locked up. Is it some kind of scandal, then, some man of the soldiers has trysted with her?"

I laughed at the idea, and then I did not know. Would he go the same at a woman, that narrow-eyed man, as he'd gone at me? I did not know. He would do anything he pleased. I could not see into the mind of such a man. I could only hope I *was* in his mind, at least now and then. I could only hope that he would want me again, want to do again what he had done with me in the forest that day.

"What, then?" said Gramshaw, slapping my arm with his jacket sleeve. "If that's so ridiculous?"

I shook my head. "I swore to the master," I said, and led Cosmos up the yard toward the trough.

Out the forest they marched at sunset and onto the moor, just glitter of tilted muskets in the dusk, then the pattern of marching legs below, then the sound of their boots, twenty-four boots, maybe, unisoned into two big ones, heavy along the road. Twelve armed men sent just to catch the one!

I stood in the loft, where I would not be bothered by anyone or begged, and all a-tremble I examined each face as the ranks passed below. There was little enough light, but I knew I would need only a glimpse, only a suggestion, I had spent so long at that man's face.

He was not among them. He was not among them, my—my darling. I wilted against the loft wall, my forehead painful against the splintery boards.

I wanted to stay hidden up there, but Gramshaw came to fetch me to the kitchen, and I thought perhaps if I ate I would feel less crushed and unbalanced, less caught in a nightmare.

"You are not going to tell us what this is all about?" Cook slapped my stew down so that it swayed in the bowl.

"I am *not allowed*," I said. "Mr. Bracken expressly forbade it."

They left me alone; worse, they turned their backs on me, some putting together the story themselves as it came through from the front of the house on the lips of maid or man. The soldiers had filled the front room and were drinking the master's ale in good quantities, and all for free, unless money had changed hands when the captain consulted with Bracken in his study. They were quiet, steady drinkers. "You'd hardly know they were here," Callie said, cocking her head at the kitchen door.

"Well, they is, and they wants bread and sausage, is the word." Cook thrust a board of just such at her, to take out.

After that silent and sinister meal they went all through the house in their boots, and soon the chambermaid Daisy Spanner arrived down among us, near speechless with excitement. She said—she could hardly get the words out—she said that they had dragged Miss Bess's bed close to her window, and bound the miss herself to standing against the foot-frame of it, and bound one of the muskets to point up under her chin, and opened the shutters and the window, and put two musketeers to kneel either side.

"And where is all the others?" said Gramshaw.

"At each and every western window," says Daisy, squirming as if she might wet herself with the thrill of it all. "Who are they awaiting?"

Many looks of dislike came my way at that. "Only one of us knows," said Cook very precisely, "and he is not saying."

"And the mistress!" Daisy remembered. "She was weeping over Miss Bess, in her own bedchamber, but now there is soldiers in it, and she've gone to a back bedroom, and locked herself in until it is over and the man in irons, whoever he is!"

"Yes, whoever he is," Cook says weightily over her shoulder toward me.

I spooned up the last of my stew and consoled myself by thinking of him, that fine creature. If I could not have my soldier back, I would settle for such a man as the highwayman, sheathed in velvet and leather and doeskin, trimmed with lace and spurs, a spray of dark feathers in that slant-brimmed hat of his. Or unsheathed, untrimmed, kissing or abusing me in the forest, sighing soft or growling filth into my ear.

Well, *she* should not have him, at least. Miserably I pushed my bowl away and sat composing myself to leave. She will be lucky to have him so much as touch a tip of her hair again.

She's had more than that before, though, my self sneered to me. *Where have they been meeting?* I wonder. *How much of him has she tasted thus far? Is it only kisses—how could he* want *those, her kisses so soft, her lips so smooth and yielding—or is there more? Are they married in secret? Does she carry his child?*

The whole inn and around were subdued that night, all custom turned away. Time crept past, increment by smallest increment. It was like being stretched on the rack, waiting for some bone to crack, some tight-pulled skin to burst. The wind had died and the moon sailed serene in a clear sky, making a cold, slow moonlight on the moor below, where the road curved around and then hoisted itself over the hill and ran at us, empty, empty. I could hardly believe what I had wrought, this silence, this ill will, this house bristling with armaments, the weeping mistress, the whispering servants.

I lay in my loft bed, listening. Hour on hour I was tensed there, mistaking my heartbeats for hoof strikes. And then when all the rigidity had exhausted me, right on the midnight as he had said, I heard it unmistakably, a little *tlot-tlot!* like a toy horse, a horse sound made by a child's mouth as he gallops a stick around a field or a wooden toy across a table.

"God save him!" Up I leaped and was at the window.

Gramshaw rustled out the straw and joined me. "Is that your man?"

He was a rag of the forest, detaching onto the road; he was a bit of blown cloth, black under the moon. "Oh God, oh God!" I moaned. He was galloping fast, but he seemed to crawl along the distant curve of road. He disappeared behind the hill and it was as if he had never been, as if my ears and eyes had deceived me and we were all still waiting on the rack.

But then he rode up, over the hill's brow, and now I could tell the flying coat from the black body low against the mare's neck. I fancied I could see the feathers on his hat, the glitter of the brooch there, the black stroke of the sheathed rapier against the horse's dark hide.

"Oh, you are a dead man," Gramshaw crooned to him at the glass beside me.

A musket shot burst the ducks off the pond. A spray of other birds squawked from their roosts out the trees.

"Shite!" said Gramshaw. We bent to the window again. The horseman galloped the other way now, and frantically. "What'd they shoot *now* for? Look, he've got away. Of course. What were they thinking?" Horse and rider shrank along the road. "He must've turned that mare on a single hoof, don't you think? Did you see him? Lucky not to unseat himself."

"What *were* they thinking? Didn't they want to lure him right up? Why, he never had a chance even to see Miss Bess and what they done to her."

"Mebbe they got impatient. Mebbe one went off by accident."

As we waited for him to show beyond the hill again, uproar began from the house. First the captain shouted enragement. Then he stopped abruptly, and the mistress screamed, wildly and on and on, and then fell to screaming weeping. I had never heard a sound so close to madness. Then Bracken. Then the captain shouted orders, and doors banged. Gramshaw and I stood either side of our window, listening down through the stable. He stared at me; he didn't know what was happening and nor did I; he didn't know if he ought to be my friend or my foe.

There were clattering thuds below on the stable door. "Rifle butts," hissed Gramshaw, and his eyes grew even wider. "What are they shouting?"

" 'Tom Coyne, Tom Coyne!' is what they are shouting," I said very faintly.

He blanched for me, bit his lip. "You better go down, then," he said. "It would not do to try running."

Somehow I got down the loft ladder without breaking my neck, and I ran along.

Crash, crash, went the door ahead of me. "Tom Coyne! Tom Coyne! Wake up! Come out!" How many soldiers were they? Some of the horses hoisted themselves from sleeping to standing in their stalls.

"I am coming, I am coming!" I cried. Did the soldiers hear me? I only had a stable-boy voice, not one for shouting charges and commands. "Hush, Cosmos," for he had whinnied out at me, and he was the most likely to rear and break himself trying to kick his way out.

I rattled the bolt so they would stop their crashing.

I opened the door. There were two of them.

"Captain wants you." They spoke and took hold of me, both at the same time.

"I will come! I will walk! There's no need to drag me." But they dragged me; clearly they were in the mood for dragging. I kicked-walked ridiculous across the cobbled yard, staggered into the kitchen past the nightgowned and shawled cook and maids with their hands to their faces. Mrs. Bracken's awful weeping was still going; there was no door closed between me and wherever she was in the house, and as they dragged me—it was a kind of painful flying that I did, all shinbones on stair-edges—as they dragged me up, the weeping echoed around my head the way bells echo in a church tower, like to send a man mad, it's said.

Mrs. Bracken was not in the room they brought me to. Bracken, when he saw me, cried, distraught, "Oh Tom, help them if you can!" and pushed out past me and my men. "That blackguard! That blackguard!" he went, along the hall outside, breaking to tears.

They set me on my feet. It was Miss Bess's chamber. She hung in her bonds at the foot of the bed. Her head was shot open at the top, and the ball had carried matter to the ceiling, had finely sprayed blood all around the room. The bed curtains, the white breeches of the soldiers standing pale and at attention by one wall, the captain's face that was shouting at me—all were speckled, were tinily beaded, with the dark of it.

Through a kind of fog I appreciated that the captain was embarrassed, that he felt someone must pay for his embarrassment, that those two by the wall had paid some—one had the captain's red slap print on his cheek—and that the stable-boy who had started the thing was as good a point of extraction as any. I let him run on while I absorbed the sights of the room. I walked forward, to where I could see all the blood spread down like a fringed red cloth across Miss Bess's bosom, and her thumb, her own thumb that had done this, still pressed on the musket's trigger.

I did not faint, exactly, but time did strange things then, leaping, dragging. Patches of sound went missing, so that the captain's words went senseless as cawing crows. I stayed quite calm, and slowly put together the scene and sequence of what had happened, and then it ran slowly forward under its own power and showed me the likely consequence.

"I think you have only to wait, sir," I said when

the time seemed right to speak.

"To wait," the captain said, with deepest scorn.

"He doesn't know yet," I said, eyeing Miss Bess's thumb to keep from facing the captain's reddened rage. "He just thinks you have taken a potshot at him, one of your soldiers. But when he hears of this, that it is *her* . . ."

I looked her up and down, awestruck again. What love might make a person do! What it might make this girl do, Bess Bracken of Bracken's Inn! There was more to her than I had thought. There was more to her than I'd known *anyone* contained inside them.

"Yes?" snapped the captain. "What then?"

"He will shoot himself, sir, and save you the trouble. And if not, I should think he'll return for revenge on you."

"Or he might go to ground!" The captain waved his speckled hand and dipped his speckled head at me. "He might for all intents and purposes disappear from the face of the earth! And never be seen again!" He finished with a ghastly smile, goggling at me.

"I think not." I could see the highwayman rising in his stirrups, in the cloak and tangle of her dark hair, in the glitter of his own glamour, almost a-swoon with it. "As you can see," I said to Miss Bess's thumb, "they were mortal fond of each other."

I had just lifted a shovelful of dung when I heard the shot. Then another shot, then another, and Gramshaw and I were at our respective box doors, each with our loaded shovel and still shots sounding, light little cracks under the dawn in the distance, not at all like the midnight blast that had near blown us off our footing in the hayloft with surprise.

"I'm going," said Gramshaw, and he dropped his shovel and closed Star's stall and ran.

And I was after him. God, it was good to run, after the night holed up and waiting, after the tenseness and the gossip-muttering and then the horrors one upon the next. I ran and I passed Gramshaw and then it became a race, until we reached the brow of the hill and could see the played-out event, when we slowed to a ragged walk side by side.

He lay in the white road, one leg crooked up. He held the rapier in one hand, still brandishing it even dead, and a pistol lay a little way from the other, silver in the dust. His fine mount was distant now, nearly to the forest, galloping mad.

"Oh, I thought that was all blood," panted Gram-shaw. "But it is his coat."

Soldiers were coming out of cover; they made little watchful runs at the body, or strolled more upright and confident behind more tentative others. He did not move; he lay and looked at the sky. His lovely hat had bowled away and lay in the weeds like some other killed creature. A chill and stammering breeze, doubtful as the slow-dawning day, made the lace at his throat signal and signal—*Here I am! Here!* A gentle-manly lock of hair trailed up from his head and danced about on the gravel.

Down into the hill shadow I walked, with Gram-shaw following. My steps felt exceedingly long but did not seem to convey me far each one. I kept on. Soldiers' white legs, black boots, were all around him; soldiers crouched at his head, at his feet, and rose again; sol-diers' voices moved time along, word by half-audible word.

"You have him!" cried Gramshaw heartily.

"No," said one of them. "He runned orf into the bushes. What's it look like?"

They made room for us, though, and we stood by the blood that was puddling by his head, where the lock of hair was caught now and fighting to pull free from the sogging.

"Dashing feller," says Gramshaw, while the dead man stared through us wide-eyed, still mad with rage, his lips pulled back from his teeth.

"I drank a very nice claret once, just this color." A soldier kicked the hem of the coat over to show the velvet side. "A Frannitch one. And I had the vineyarder's wife along wi' it."

The captain dropped his heavy hand on my shoulder. "I should never have doubted you, lad," he said at my other ear. "You knew what you was talking about."

"Yer," said someone nastily. "Any more of these lawless fiends you is apprised the where'bouts of, the movements?"

"No," I said, noting the many darknesses where the fine clothes were spoiled, where a ball had gone in and blood and bone shards had come out. "No, I cannot help you further than this."

"Oh, I don't know. You could bring us a horse, now, couldn't he, captain? Any old nag will do, to fetch this chap to Chafton and show the constable. Just summink to sling 'im over, like. Think your master would begrudge us a borry?"

I looked at the captain.

"It's not put the nicest way," he said, "but yes, Tom Coyne, that would be most helpful."

"Come, Gramshaw." I turned from the sights.

"Good lad!"

"What a courteous chap!"

"En't people frenly 'roun' these parts?"

So the soldiers jeered quietly behind us.

"*You* can go to Chafton," I said to Gramshaw when we were out of their hearing.

"To Chafton?" I might have asked him to go to London, or maybe across the water to Frannishland, he sounded so astonished.

"To fetch back Saxifrage when she have carried the man in."

"But I went yesterday for you! And this would be on foot!"

"That's right," I said. "But there is only so many forms of torture a man can take. And I have had them all, these two nights and a day."

Which, as he had given me some of them, and even though he ranked above me in the stables and could have refused, I trusted him to understand.

He walked awhile, looking side-on at me as if I

were perhaps a more interesting specimen of person than hitherto he had thought. We come-upped the hilltop then, and the sun burst upon us and showed me to him, all glare and hay scraps as I was. Its warmth painted my front but did not reach farther into the body of me, which was all cold knowledge. Bosomy Bess with her tumble of scented hair and that grand audacious man risen in his stirrups and reaching for her—I had killed them both, sure as if I had pulled the triggers myself. And all for hope of a glimpse that I did not gain, of a king's man, of my man and my darling, that I might never see again nor touch. Two souls were dead of that secret, of that meeting and mixing of men in the dark of the forest, of that madness. Such weighty other sins, now, were piled upon the original that the joy of it and the glory had been pinched right out, as sudden as a candle flame between an inn man's fingertips.

"What you staring at?" I said to Gramshaw, and the smoke of the extinguishment poured black out my throat and my eyes.

"Fair enough." He turned his mild face toward Bracken's. "I'll go to Chafton, then, if you want."

FINGERNAIL

·

BY WILLIAM SLEATOR

I met Bernard in the fertility symbol room of the National Museum in Bangkok.

I went to other rooms before that, and saw many old and beautiful things—I am a poor boy from the countryside and never been to a museum before, and people told me this one was good. And then I go into this room and nothing is there but cocks in glass cases, made out of stone and metal and wood, many size and many shape.

And also in the room is a *farang*, a westerner, very handsome man with light yellow hair and dark blue eyes. I have seen many *farangs* in Bangkok, but I never know one. He keeps looking at me, and I keep looking at him—I am not shy. And this *farang*, when he sees me looking, he comes right over to me and kisses me. Right there in the museum! People are walking by, but no one sees.

I am very surprised. Twenty years old, and already

have sex with a Thai woman and a few Thai men, but nobody ever kiss me before. I walk out of the museum fast. The *farang* follows me. I cross the street through the cars stuck in traffic and he crosses the street too. I walk past Sanam Luang, the big empty field near the Grand Palace. The *farang* comes after me now. We stop by a tuk-tuk, little three-wheel taxi. He lights a cigarette.

The *farang* cannot speak Thai and I cannot speak English. But we can make sign to each other. He makes sign he wants to have sex together. I make sign saying, "No, no, no!" Then he makes sign we can eat together. I am hungry. I never know a *farang* before. I make sign saying, "Yes!"

The *farang* is very happy and smiles a very big smile. We ride in tuk-tuk to the *farang*'s hotel, near the big old train station, Hua Lampong. We go to a restaurant outside the hotel. I never have enough money to eat in restaurant. I eat duck with rice, very delicious. The *farang* smokes many cigarettes. The waiter speaks English and of course Thai, so he can speak with me and with the *farang*, and tell us what the other one is saying. The *farang* is French, but he speaks English too. He is thirty-two years old. His name is Bernard Duval. I tell him my name is Lep, which means "fingernail."

He wants me to come to his room after we eat, but I cannot, I have to go back to the school where I work and where I live. He wants me to meet him at the hotel the next day at lunchtime, but I cannot, I have to work then. I say I cannot come until six o'clock tomorrow evening. He says he will wait for me until then. He smiles and takes my hand when I leave.

I come from a small village in the countryside. I went to school for only four years, because my family is so poor and I have to work, taking care of the buffalo. When I was seventeen I went to Bangkok and worked in construction for my older brother. I am short, but already I am strong from working in the village. And from working in construction I am stronger. But my brother doesn't pay me, so I find another job, working in a school, helping the cook to make food for the students. Their families are rich and they have enough money to go to school for many years, but I am not envy, I am lucky to have work, this is my life. I have another job too, working for a very rich titled lady, a *Khunying*, taking care of her cars and her garden.

And now I am very excited. I never knew a *farang* before and this one seems very kind, smiling a lot, speaking gently, buying delicious food for me. He is also very handsome. Maybe something will happen. Maybe this will be something good for my life.

I am so excited I even have trouble sleeping, but never mind. I get up at three the next morning to go to the market. I have to go early because later there will be too much traffic and it will take me too long. I buy food and I carry it back to the school and I help the cook to cut things up, many many onions, and pounding all the garlic and chilies for a long time. I help serve it to all the students and then I clean everything up. After that I go to the *Khunying*'s house and I wash four of her cars, and then I do some work in the garden, cutting the grass with clippers. After that I hurry back to the school to the little place where I sleep next to the staff toilet and I take shower and put on my best clothes and take the bus downtown to the restaurant. I want to be on time so the *farang* will not think I am not coming, but I am still ten minutes late. I am afraid the *farang* will be angry but he is not, he smiles and says, "Hello Lep," and I say, "Hello Bernard." And then we go up to his room.

I've never been in a room like this, with a western bathroom and a big high bed and a thick carpet and a

TV. But I don't have time to look at the room, because Bernard is kissing me. And I am learning how to kiss him.

It was never like this before, the kissing, slowly taking our clothes off, doing many things, taking our time. Before, with Thai men, it was always fast and secret, hurry up so no one will catch us. Here, with Bernard, no one can catch us. Here, with Bernard, we can do anything we want, for as long as we want. We can study every part of our bodies. I can tell he likes my body, and my dark skin. His body is very strong too, from karate, he says, and his skin is very white. And the kissing! The kissing makes everything different. This is not just a quick release, the way Thai people do it. The kissing and the taking time make it meaning. Now I know that for me the real way is with a man, not with a woman.

Because already I love Bernard.

Nobody was ever so good with me, understanding my body so well. We do many things. We stay in bed for a long time. He strokes my body, smoking a cigarette. Finally we fall asleep in each other's arms.

When I wake up in the dark I can see from the clock by the bed that it is time for me to hurry and go to the market. I want to say good-bye to Bernard, but I don't want to disturb him and wake him up. But when I pull away from him he comes awake. He reaches out to pull me back. I point at the clock and signal to him that I have to go to work. He kisses me and then gets dressed and comes down with me, smoking a cigarette.

I don't understand until we go to the restaurant with the English-speaking waiter, which is open very late. Bernard and I had no trouble understanding each other in bed, but we have a lot of trouble understanding about practical things. And he has something important to tell me: He has to go back to France today!

Now I am very sad. But Bernard keeps smiling and telling me he will never forget me. He asks me if I want to learn French or English. I say English, because I know it is the most important language in the world. He writes down his address in English letters. I write down the address of the school; the waiter, who is very smart, writes it in English for Bernard.

Bernard says he will write to me every week, and he will come back to Thailand to see me as soon as he can. Outside, on the dark street, he kisses me. He gives me money to take a taxi. I want to save the money and take the bus, but Bernard waves at a taxi, and I get in. I watch him out of the back window as the taxi drives away, and he stands there smoking and watching me.

I am very tired all day, but it is a good tired. I work every day, and on Friday I get paid. On Saturday I go to the weekend market at Sanam Luang, and buy an English-Thai/Thai-English dictionary. I also buy a book called *Seventy-nine Hours*—after you study this book for seventy-nine hours, you will be able to speak English. The bookseller says it is a very good book, it really works. I have almost no money from my salary after I buy the books, but I don't care. I can eat at the school. And what else do I need money for? Now I can study.

More than anything else I wanted to go to school, but I could go for only four years. And after that I had to work very hard so I had no time to study on my own. But now, because of Bernard, I have a very strong reason to study. I can find the time now. I work with the book *Seventy-nine Hours*. Every week a letter comes from Bernard, and I read it, using the dictionary. At first it is very hard, but slowly I begin to understand. I learn English from the book and also from Bernard's letters. And every week I write back to Bernard. My English writing looks very stupid, very different from his. And he writes back that he doesn't understand one word in my first letters, I am writing too many things backward. But I keep writing, thinking of him all the time. And after a while he writes that he can understand more things in my letters now. He never forgets to write to me, and that is why I keep studying harder and harder.

Every time, we write how much we love each other.

Sometimes I have quick sex with Thai men, a release only. But not kissing, not loving like with Bernard. Not the same thing at all.

And after ten months I get the best letter of all. Bernard is coming back to Thailand in one month. I will see him very soon!

I have already finished the book *Seventy-nine Hours*. I talk as much as possible with the English teacher at the school. He helps me say the words right. He can hardly believe that Lep, the cook's helper, can speak English like this now. I can't wait to talk to Bernard. He doesn't know from my letters how well I can speak English. We will really be able to understand each other now.

His airplane arrives at nine o'clock in the evening, so I am free to meet him. I take the slow hot bus all the way out to the airport in the traffic. I have never been to the airport before, but I am good at finding my way around. Inside, I wait behind the fence with all the crowds of other people waiting for someone to come from another country. I watch the immigration door. I am very excited.

Bernard comes through the door, looking so lovely. I jump up and down and wave at him. He sees me right away and throws a kiss to me. I run to the place where he can come out from inside the fence. We hug each other very strong. I never want to let go of him. But we are in the airport so we have to pull away.

He will be very happy to hear how well I speak English! I pick up his bags and smile and say, "Welcome to Thailand, sir. I hope you had a very comfortable flight."

His smile falls away. "Where did you learn to speak like that?" he asks me, looking very serious. "Who taught you that word 'comfortable'?"

"I learn from my book, *Seventy-nine Hours*, and from your letters," I say, holding on to his bags, a little frightened now. "I learn many words from the dictionary. Is in my pocket now. I write to you about it."

"Are you sure?" he asks me, his eyes very thin. "Are you sure you didn't learn from another *farang* while I was away?"

I don't know what he's talking about. But I am very unhappy because something is wrong. "I don't have any other *farang* friends, you know that," I tell him. "The English teacher at the school helps me. I don't understand what is problem." And then I say very softly, "I love you." It is the first time I can say it to him.

He is still looking at me very serious. But then his face gets soft and kind again. He smiles and touches my face. "Oh, Lep, I'm sorry," he says. "I was just surprised about how you speak English. Come on, let's go. I don't want to waste any time."

In the taxi we hold hands and sit very close and talk about how much we miss each other. Talking is delicious. At the hotel we go right up to his room. Now we are impatient. He pulls my clothes off very fast and I pull off his. And tonight it is better than the first time, almost one year ago. Tonight we can say, "I love you," and many other things too. And tonight is Saturday, so I don't have to work tomorrow at the school or at the *Khunying*'s house. We don't get out of bed until lunchtime on Sunday.

We eat lunch in the restaurant and we talk, talk, talk. If I don't understand, I look in the dictionary. Now I can tell him about my life. "Very unfair that you can't go to school, someone as smart as you who can learn English so well, so quickly," he says.

I think from his voice maybe he is not happy that I am smart, but I tell myself I imagine it. I smile and lift my shoulders. "This is my life," I say. "And my English not very good yet."

He tells me about his life. He lives with his mother in a small house very far away from Paris. He works building the railroad track. He talks a lot about karate, how he goes to class every day, and now he can wear a black belt.

"It is very important to you to fight with other people?" I ask him, joking.

"No, not that. I do it because it makes me feel good, and to stay in shape." He lights another cigarette.

After lunch we go to walk in the park, where there are many tall trees, and flowers, and a big lake. "But this is not like the real jungle, where my village is," I tell him.

"Someday I would like to go to your village," he says.

"I will be proud to take you there." I am very happy he wants to go, and not only because I want to show him. I also don't have enough money to go by myself—I have not been back to see my family and friends since I came to Bangkok four years ago.

Then I have to go to the toilet very bad. I know where it is, because when I am not studying I come to the park on my days off. "I have to go to the toilet. You can see it over there," I tell him, pointing. "I have to hurry. I meet you there."

I run to the toilet. Then inside I have to wait for somebody else to finish. He takes a long time. Finally I can go. I take a long time too. At last I come out.

Bernard is standing there waiting. He has the same very serious frowning face he had at the airport. "Who did you have sex with in there?" he says.

"Huh?" I say, not understanding.

"Sex. S. E. X. Look it up in your precious dictionary. You should know the word. You're always looking for it."

Now I understand. "Bernard, why you think I want to do that when I am with you?" I lower my voice. "I love you."

"Easy to say that. Not so easy to explain why you were in the toilet for so long. Was he Thai or *farang*?" He lifts his hand. "Never mind. I don't want to know." He turns and walks away.

I feel like crying, except I already use up all my tears when I am a child. I hurry after him. I reach for his arm. "Bernard, I have to wait a long time for somebody else. Then it takes me a—"

He pushes my hand away. "I can hear in your voice you are lying."

People are looking at us, but I don't care. Now I am angry too. I grab his elbow and pull him around very hard to face me. "Stop it!" I shout at him. I know it is wrong to speak so loud in public, but I forget that now. "Stop being crazy man! You are imagine everything!" I lower my voice again. "After so many times with you last night, and you are right here waiting, you think I do that with another? *Baa!*" I say, meaning "crazy" in Thai.

Bernard's mouth opens. His eyes are wide. Then he puts a hand over them and shakes his head. "Oh, Lep, my darling Lep," he whispers, choking. He sounds like he is going to cry. "I'm sorry. I love you too much, that is the problem. Come back to the hotel with me. I have to hold you. Now."

And back at the hotel it is even more passion than before, because first we were fighting, and now we are making up. Bernard has tears in his eyes while we make love. And afterward we sit together at the desk and he helps me with my English writing. He is a very gentle teacher, not like the teachers at my village school where they hit you when you make a mistake.

Every evening as soon as I am free I come to be with Bernard. I sleep with him at the hotel and get up at three to go to the market. We have sex all the time. We talk a lot. We eat together. He helps me with my English. I get almost no sleep. I have never been so happy.

Bernard tells me he really wants to go to my village—he has never been outside of Bangkok. And I am very proud to bring him to my home. So on the next weekend I get Saturday off from the *Khunying*—of course I will lose the pay, even though she is very, very rich. On Friday after work we take the overnight train to Surin, and then the bus to my village in the morning. We can stay there for one night.

Everybody is very impressed that I am with this tall rich *farang*. The babies cry when they see Bernard; they have never seen white skin before and think he is a ghost. Bernard is very polite. He has no problem using the Thai toilet or showering outside in his underpants with a basin and dipper or sleeping on a mat on the floor in the same room with everybody else. In the village Bernard is not jealous because he can see very clear that here, men never have sex with men, they cannot imagine it. So, of course, we cannot do it in the village. When we get back to the hotel in Bangkok on Sunday night we fall into each other's arms.

Bernard has to go back to France the next Sunday. On the Saturday night before he leaves we go to a big disco. Here, women dance with women and men can dance together too! Bernard has never seen me dance before and he is very surprised to see that I dance very good, very funny and smiling, and I make up many steps. People stop dancing to watch me.

Then I have to go to the toilet. I run upstairs fast and go quickly and come down fast, remembering about the park. At first I can't find Bernard when I come down. Then I see him at the bar, drinking whiskey. Normally he doesn't drink it. I sit beside him and he orders more whiskey, and smokes one cigarette after the other. "Bernard, I come back form the toilet very fast," I say.

"Did you?" He lifts his shoulders and takes a big drink of whiskey. When I ask him what is wrong he says nothing is wrong. He will not talk about it. I am very sad because this is our last night together. Soon we leave the disco. When we go to find a taxi he walks like a snake—he is very drunk. I ask him many times what is wrong and all he will say is, "Nothing." I tell him this is our last night together, but he acts like he doesn't care. Back at the hotel he will not let me touch him. He drinks the whiskey in the room and smokes cigarettes. And even though I am very worried and unhappy, I still go right to sleep, because I have been sleeping very little in all these two weeks.

I wake up when I feel something pressing down very hard on my face—Bernard, pushing a pillow down against my head. I can't breathe!

Bernard is strong from karate. But I am very strong from working on the farm and working in construction—especially strong in my legs. I lift both feet and put them next to Bernard's stomach and then I kick, with all the strength in my legs. The air comes out of Bernard's mouth and he drops the pillow and falls backward off the bed onto the floor. He sits there on the floor with his back against the wall, trying to breathe.

Then he leans forward and cries and cries and cries. I have never seen anybody cry like this. Tears are running down his face and making the carpet dark. And even he just try to kill me I still love him. I don't really understand why, except that for me love is a very strong feeling, stronger than anger and fear. I go over and sit beside him and put my arms around him. He holds on to me very tight. He can barely talk, he is crying so hard, but he tells me it was the way people were watching me dancing, and many follow me up to the toilet. He says he is sorry he is so crazy, he has never loved anyone as much as me.

And then we make love right there on the carpet on the floor. This time it is more passion than ever before—because Bernard just try to kill me.

He leaves the next day. He gives me his picture and I keep it in my wallet. He tells me in many letters how sorry he is, how much he loves me. I write back that I love him more than before. It is true.

I work at the school, I work for the *Khunying*. I study English with another book, more difficult, so I can speak better with Bernard. I write to Bernard often. I tell him I love only him: I miss him so much, he is always on my mind. And I tell him when is school vacation. He writes back that he can't wait to see me, he will take time off work to come sooner, he will come when is school vacation. We can go away together!

And finally Bernard comes back to Thailand for the third time, just when I have my vacation from the job at the school. We go to a beautiful island in Malaysia, Pulao Tioman. We live in a thatched bungalow on the beach. It rains and rains, but we don't care, we are making love in the bungalow, day and night. When we don't make love, Bernard helps me with English.

On the last night it is not raining and we go to a bar on the beach, and drink with the men from the island. I am happy, I forget, and I dance. The men clap for me. Bernard keeps drinking.

That night in the bungalow, naked, Bernard smashes a whiskey bottle and tries to cut my neck. I tell him, "No, Bernard, don't do this!" but he will not stop, he pushes the broken bottle at my neck. I reach out fast and squeeze his balls, so very hard that he screams and drops the bottle and cuts his foot. He cries and cries while I clean and bind his foot, he says he is so sorry, so sorry, he loves me too much. And then we make love. Very passion—always special passion after Bernard tries to kill me, because we have terrible fight and then we make up. I feel passion too. I love him too.

But now I know Bernard is crazy. And I am beginning to be afraid of him.

Big storm next day, and the regular ferry is canceled. But we cannot wait, because Bernard has to catch a plane in Bangkok the next day to get back to work on time. We take a small fishing boat in the storm, with many other people. Very crowded, very rough water, and everybody is throwing up for six hours. Everybody but Bernard and me. We sit on the deck in the rain with our arms around each other, talking and laughing. I am thinking maybe I can forgive him, even he try to kill me two times.

We take the train from Kuala Lumpur to Penang, from Penang to Bangkok. At Penang we have to get off the train and do customs. Many people, long lines. While we wait, I talk to some Thai students. They see me with Bernard and ask me about the handsome *farang*; I tell them we are very good friends, on holiday together. They think I am very lucky.

On the train again, Bernard is not talking. He is angry. But I know he cannot kill me on the train in front of all the other people. So I close my eyes to sleep, hoping he will not be angry any more when I wake up.

When I wake up Bernard is gone. I wait, but he does not come back from the toilet. I look all over the train. He is not in the toilet. He is not on the train.

Then I feel my pocket and the breath goes out of me. My passport is gone. My heart starts to beat very strong. My wallet is gone, with all my money and my ID card and Bernard's picture.

Now I understand, and my heart goes hard. Bernard was jealous because I was talking to the Thai students. He took my wallet and my passport and got off the train, leaving me alone, with nothing. Lucky we are already in Thailand and I don't have to go through immigration.

This time I cannot forgive Bernard. I cannot love him now. When he try to kill me he was drunk, not thinking, not in control. But this time he is not drunk, very in control, very thinking. What he do this time is worse.

In Bangkok it takes me very long time to get new passport, new ID card, especially because I have no money. I have to walk everywhere, and Bangkok is very big. Letters from Bernard come to the school, but I do not open them, I throw them away. When I finally get new passport and new ID card, I try to find new job. I don't want Bernard to know where I live. And I think maybe I can get better job, more money, now that I can speak English because of Bernard.

I get a job as a bartender, easier work and more money. The owner likes me because I speak English with a French accent, he says. The bar is on a street with many bars where girls dance on platforms in swimsuits and wear numbers. Many *farangs* come and drink, and if a *farang* likes a girl, he pay the bar and she has to go with him.

The customers like me, because I make many jokes with them in English and we all laugh a lot. Sometimes I get up on the platform and dance, not for work like the girls, but for fun. The customers like this very much. They call me, "Lep the dancing bartender." More customers come because of me. The owner sees this, and he pay me more money.

Now I have my own room to live in, and many friends, and a new life.

And one customer tells another, and another tells another, about me. And one night a *farang* comes to the bar who works for the English newspaper in Bangkok. He does not come for the girls, he comes to meet me. He is not as handsome as Bernard. I do not fall in love with him in one night, like with Bernard. For many days we just talk in English, about everything. He loves to talk to me and thinks I am very smart and writes down many things I say.

And after we know each other for a month, we

finally sleep together. By the time we do, we know we love each other. It is a deeper feeling than the love I had for Bernard. This time it is real.

He is not jealous, he is not crazy like Bernard.

We are building a house in my village. I was always the poorest, and now I have the most beautiful house. I have everything that I ever dreamed of in my life.

Sometimes I think about Bernard and I wonder: How could I imagine I love someone who is so crazy? And then I think: Where will I be now, if I never knew him?

DYKE MARCH

·

BY ARIEL SCHRAG

THE MISSING PERSON

·

BY JENNIFER FINNEY BOYLAN

That was the summer I gave up on being a boy, and became a girl instead. Most people didn't notice the difference, because it wasn't a matter of what I wore, or even how I acted. But something changed in my heart that year, and never changed back.

I didn't know the word *transgendered* back then, and even after I learned the word it would be years and years before I could say it out loud. But the summer between eighth and ninth grades I knew that somehow I had left the world of boys for good, and began slowly, blindly, feeling my way toward the world of women.

We'd moved that June into a house in Devon, Pennsylvania, a town famous for its weeklong horse show and country fair. For the last week of May and the first week of June, Devon was filled with men and women wearing jodhpurs and carrying riding crops, open jumpers, hunters, and the Budweiser Clydesdales. Women in long dresses sat in the backs of antique horse-drawn carriages, and as I stood in the front yard of our house, I watched as they rolled down the street away from me and waved good-bye.

People said our house was haunted, that a girl who had drowned in the 1920s floated through the hallways, or paced around and around in the attic. The bedroom that I was sleeping in had been hers, a long time ago.

In the summertime I kept all of the windows open in my room, and sometimes late at night I'd hear, on the street outside, the sound of a single rider approaching, the hooves clopping ominously as the horse drew nearer and nearer.

Other times, I heard—or imagined that I could hear—the sound of small footsteps going around and around in a circle on the floor of the attic over my head.

My dog, Sausage—a fat, demented Dalmatian—raised her head and listened to the footsteps and growled.

You know who that is, Sausage? I said to the dog. *That's somebody who isn't really there.*

The dog nodded. Sausage had a pretty good sense of what the deal was. *Somebody who isn't really there?* the dog said. *You mean—someone like you?*

That was the same summer that some friends of my parents—the Reynoldses—welcomed an exchange student named Li Fung into their house. Li Fung came from Taiwan and had come to America in order to study English.

She'd been at the Reynoldses' house for only a few days, though, when she suddenly disappeared. She'd gone up to her room before dinner one night, locked the door, and vanished.

When the Reynoldses called her down for dinner, there was no response, and with a sense of rising panic, they banged on her door. Mr. Reynolds eventually kicked the door open with his foot, sending the deadbolt skittering across the room.

When they entered Li Fung's bedroom, they found her shoes placed neatly together at the foot of her bed. Her window—like me, she lived on the third floor of an old, supposedly haunted house—was closed. The closet door, which held the very few articles of clothing Li Fung had brought with her from Taiwan, was slightly ajar. On her bed, open and facedown, was a copy of a book called *Jonathan Livingston Seagull*.

The police were called in, including a pair of

detectives who checked the room for signs of forced entry. There were none. No one had propped a ladder up and climbed to the third floor and hauled her off; no one had tampered with the lock. Li Fung had simply gone up to her room and turned to steam.

Sometimes I considered the mystery of Li Fung as I lay in my bed listening to the soft creak of footsteps from the attic or the clop of horses' hooves on the street. It seemed to me that the secret of the disappearance lay in the open copy of *Jonathan Livingston Seagull* that had been left upon her bed. My theory? She'd fallen into the book.

I knew it was a tragedy and everything; and there was no doubt that the Reynoldses, whom I'd see in the days to come drinking gin in our black living room with my parents, had been fundamentally unraveled by the turn of events. But there was a part of me that was resentful of Li Fung as well, just dissolving into nothing like that. To me it seemed she'd taken the easy way out.

I woke up to hear my mother yelling. I checked my clock. It was after midnight.

"You promised you'd be back by ten," my mother said. "You gave me your word!"

"I'm sorry," said Lydia, my older sister. "I didn't want to worry you."

"I've been worried sick!" said my mother.

"I was fine."

They were standing in the hallway, my mother in her doorway, my sister in hers, having at it. My sister was wearing a hippie skirt. Sometimes, when no one was home, I stole her skirt out of the hamper and wore it while I read a book in my room. But it looked better on her than it did on me.

"You could have been dead somewhere. Killed!"

"Mother, stop being so paranoid!"

"You lied to me!" my mother shouted.

"Can we not talk about this now?" my sister said. "Jesus Christ!"

"Don't use that tone of voice with me!"

"Then stop nagging me!"

"You're grounded, for two weeks!" my mother shouted.

"Go to hell!" Lydia shouted, and slammed her door. For a while I lay there in the dark, wondering what was going to happen to my sister.

In the morning, my mother was sitting at the table by herself, drinking coffee.

"What was all that shouting last night?"

"What shouting?" said my mother.

"You and Lydia," I said. "Going at it like that."

"We were just having a discussion," my mother said. "Lydia disappointed us by staying out too late."

"How come you never give me a curfew?" I asked, which was a fair enough question. My parents never told me I had to be home by a certain time, ever.

"Well, it's different with you," said my mother generously. "You're the boy."

On the last day of the Devon Horse Show, everyone in my family mysteriously left the house. I think my father was at the hardware store, my mother at the hairdresser. I don't know where my sister was. But the only ones home were me and the dog, and the ghost of the girl who wasn't there.

I crept down the third-floor stairs, opened the hamper, and got out the hippie skirt my sister had thrown in the hamper. Then I put on a a black Danskin leotard top, applied some pale lipstick, and looked at myself in the mirror. Because of my long hair and small bones, I looked like a fairly normal fourteen-year-old girl.

From outside I heard the sounds of horses' hooves on the street.

Okay, I thought. *I'll do it.*

Sausage looked at me as I headed for the door, one of my sister's purses hanging from one shoulder. *Are you crazy?* the dog said. *Are you out of your mind?*

I nodded to the dog. *I might be*, I said.

Then I went outside, got on my brown Schwinn, and rode my bike to the Devon Horse Show.

In a plastic lawn chair sat a man in a sleeveless undershirt, drinking lemonade, listening to the Phillies game on a transistor radio. He waved at me as I sped past.

I locked the bike and walked through the carnival gates. Before me was a large oval ring where girls in hard hats rode green hunters. To the right was the ornate Victorian grandstand, filled with men and women in straw bonnets. There was the distant sound of a calliope playing "In the Good Old Summertime," the smell of buttered popcorn. Candy stripers sold lemon sticks. Boys my age walked through the teeming crowds holding foaming lavender bouquets of cotton candy. An announcer on a public address system described the progress of the equestrians. *One jump fault, two time faults. The next exhibitor is Melanie Brown, of Ghost Lantern Farm, in Chadd's Ford, Pennsylvania, riding Homin' Notime. Melanie Brown of Chadd's Ford.*

There was scattered applause from the grandstand. Ladies fanned themselves with their programs.

Overhead, the summer sun shone down on me. It was the first time in my life I had ever felt the sun on my face as a girl. I felt like someone who had been released from jail, like someone who'd spent her whole life in prison only to be unexpectedly paroled, at the age of fourteen, and set loose upon the world.

My heart pounded in my breast. *Jesus*, I thought as I walked through the unperturbed crowd. *Can't they tell?*

It didn't appear that they could.

I walked through the midway, where kids were throwing darts at balloons, squirting water guns into the mouths of plastic clowns, hurling baseballs at stacks of milk bottles. From a booth a woman in an Amish habit sold Pennsylvania Dutch funnel cakes. Above me, reaching toward the hot sun, the Ferris wheel spun around and around. The screams of girls rose and fell from the sky.

There was a sign by the Ferris wheel. IF YOU STAND HERE WHILE WHEEL IS TURNING, YOU WILL BE KILLED.

I stood by a large oak tree and watched a woman painting someone's portrait in pastels. The person she was drawing wasn't there; she was rendering the picture from a photograph. She looked at me and smiled.

"What's your name?" she said kindly.

"Jenny," I said.

I was fourteen years old, and it was the first time in my life I had spoken my name out loud.

"Are you riding in the show, Jenny?"

"No," I said.

"Oh, I could have sworn you were a rider," she said, adding color to the cheeks of the woman in her portrait. "You have that equestrian look, the red cheeks, the pageboy."

"Thank you," I said.

"I have a daughter about your age," the woman said. She wasn't looking at me now, but was focusing her attention, instead, on her work. "She used to ride. Now it's just boys, boys, boys. Do you have a boyfriend, Jenny?"

"No," I said.

She looked over at me. "Are you all right, honey?"

I nodded my head.

"You're not lost, are you?"

I didn't know what to tell her. *Yeah, I'm lost, I guess.*

I turned and ran into the crowd. I wondered, not for the last time, if stealing my sister's clothes and walking around in public had been such a good idea.

I reached the midway. Little kids were riding on the merry-go-round. It had a real steam calliope inside, which played "O Them Golden Slippers." Moms and dads stood at the edge of the railing, waving each time their little children whirled past.

"Be prepared to be amazed," said a voice.

I turned around. A man in a top hat was standing on a box. "Yes, you there, little miss. Gather 'round and witness these feats of legerdemain, guaranteed to astonish and astound."

Above him was a hand-painted banner that read, THE GREAT SCARAMUZZINO. FEATS OF MYSTERY 50¢.

I reached into my sister's purse and handed him two quarters. He put them in a cigar box on a chair by his side.

There was a guy named Sal Scaramuzzino at my middle school—a hugely fat, kind of mean guy, who lived down in South Philadelphia. At school, Sal was always offering to beat me up, a service that I usually declined. But the Scaramuzzino I knew didn't seem to have much in common with this guy. The Scaramuzzino I knew had no feats of mystery.

"Now watch carefully, little miss," he said as he waved a white silk handkerchief through the air, "as once again we demonstrate"—he stuffed the handkerchief inside his fist—"that the hand is quicker than the eye!" He opened his hand, and the handkerchief had disappeared.

There was applause behind me. The Great Scaramuzzino was drawing a crowd. There were three guys a little older than I was and two girls. The girls were wearing makeup. Their bras were not filled with socks, which is more than we could say about some people.

"And now, little miss," he said, reaching out for me with a hand covered with a white buttoned glove and spinning me by the shoulder, "we spin you once, twice, three times, we spin you, and *presto change-o*—"

He pulled a handkerchief out of my sister's purse. "The hand is quicker than the eye!" The teenagers applauded again. The Great Scaramuzzino wasn't done yet. He pulled out another handkerchief from my purse, only this one was red, and it was knotted to another, colored green. He started to pull on the hankies, and now a long chain of scarves was emerging from my purse. The magician waved them through the air. Then he stuffed them all inside a black top hat.

The Great Scaramuzzino waved a black wand over the hat, reached in, and pulled out a bouquet of roses. To my total shame, he gave them to me. Everyone applauded.

There was a boy standing next to me who had braces and bad skin. "How do you, like, think he did that?" he said, and his voice broke. I felt sorry for him. I knew how hard it was, talking to girls.

"Now let me present to you the disappearing orb," said the magician. He put what looked like an eggcup on the table before him, and placed an ovoid lid upon it. "*Presto change-o* appears the sphere of mystery." He removed the lid, and a white sphere was there. Then he put the lid back on the eggcup, waved his hands, and removed it again. The sphere was gone.

"And now, pick a card, any card," said the Great Scaramuzzino, and fanned a deck before me. I picked a card with one hand. The other was still holding the bouquet of roses.

"Without showing me the card, look at its face." I looked at it. It was the queen of diamonds. "You can show your friend as well." I showed the card to the boy next to me. He nodded and looked at me, as if the two of us were now linked, somehow, by the fact that we shared a secret.

"Now put it back in the deck," said the Great Scaramuzzino. The crowd watching the magician was growing large now. Grown-ups were watching. I felt sweat beginning to pour down my temples. I put the card in, and the Great Scaramuzzino closed and shuffled the deck.

"My name's Mark," said the boy.

"I'm Jenny," I said.

"Are you, like, here with anyone?"

"No," I said.

"Cool," said Mark, and reached out and took my hand. Mark's palm was sweaty.

"And now," the Great Scaramuzzino said. "Once again we learn. The hand is quicker than the—" He reached out toward me with his buttoned glove. Mark squeezed my hand, then softly slid his fingers up my arm toward the crook of my elbow.

I dropped the bouquet of roses, turned, and ran.

Ran past the Ferris wheel and the booth for funnel cakes and the Nether Providence Tack Shop and the press box where some of the characters from *Dark Shadows*, a television show, were handing out autographed pictures of themselves. I ran past the hamburger stand, past the pizza booth and the tree where the lady was still painting portraits in pastels. Two Pennsylvania State cops stood by the blue water barrel with their hands on their holsters. One of them looked at me closely as I sped past.

I ran out the gates and found my bicycle and pedaled for my life, heading up the hill toward home. From behind me I heard the voice of the announcer commentating the show. *All riders reverse now, all reverse.*

I got home to find my parents' car in the driveway. *They were back.*

I wondered whether it would be better, in the end, to enter the house in my sister's paisley skirt or to enter it naked. This last suggestion I discarded, but who knows? Naked actually had a lot to recommend it, compared to the other option.

My mother, I knew, would be in the kitchen. My father was probably in the basement, looking very

THE MISSING PERSON

carefully at whatever it was he'd bought at the hardware store. Drill bits and a fertilizer spreader. An electric screwdriver.

The whereabouts of my sister, whose clothes I was wearing, were unknown.

I crept around the front of the house and walked across the porch. I peeked in the door. I heard my mother in the kitchen, heard the sound of the television in the family room. I swooped through the front hall and ran up the stairs, two steps at a time, toward my room on the third floor. I got to the bathroom and locked it with a deadbolt.

There was an old wooden cabinet, badly made, in the corner of the bathroom that had a loose board in the bottom. I pulled off the loose board, and put the skirt and the blouse in the secret compartment. There was other stuff already in there. A pair of my mother's earrings. A necklace. A copy of *Seventeen* magazine, a paperback edition of *The Feminine Mystique*, which I had tried to read and did not understand. I put the loose board back in place. Then took a deep breath.

I ran some hot water in the sink and rubbed off the lipstick. I got soap on my lips, rubbed them until they were raw, then dried off with a towel.

I pulled on a pair of blue jeans and a white T-shirt and stuck my hair behind my ears, looked in the mirror. I was a boy again. My eyes filled with tears. *But I don't want this*, I whispered to my reflection. *I want to stay Jenny.*

"Jimmm-eeeee," my mother called up the stairs. "Are you up there?"

"Just a second," I answered in my boy voice.

All right, you, I said to the mirror. *Now you listen up. You're never doing this again, okay?*

I was just about to leave the bathroom when I realized I'd forgotten to put my sister's purse in the hidey-hole. It was lying on its side by the door. I pulled the loose board off the bottom of the cabinet again. Then I dumped the contents of the purse onto the floor.

It contained three dollars, some change, a tube of rose-colored lipstick, and a single playing card. *Hey,* I thought, *this isn't mine.* I picked up the card and looked at it.

Queen of diamonds.

The Great Scaramuzzino had tried to teach me that the hand was quicker than the eye, and I thought, *Okay, maybe so. But then, if you think about it, so what?*

As far as I was concerned, the eye was pretty slow.

A few days later, the Reynoldses found Li Fung.

Mrs. Reynolds had been out in her living room, dusting, when she heard a strange, soft weeping sound. At first she thought it was a bird, trapped in the wall, but it didn't sound like a bird. It was a human voice, although the words it was saying were not English. For a few moments, Mrs. Reynolds thought that Li Fung had come back to haunt her, to blame her for allowing her to vanish like that.

Then she realized that Li Fung was actually *in the wall*. She called her husband, who came home from work and knocked on the wall. Li Fung knocked back. A few minutes later, he started smashing through the wall with a sledgehammer. The old plaster of the house gave way relatively quickly. A few minutes after that, they had a hole big enough to look through. There was Li Fung, wedged between one of the support beams and some electrical wires. Plaster dust was in her hair, and her skin was black and blue. She could barely open her eyes.

"Why, Li Fung," said Mrs. Reynolds. "What in the

world are you doing in the wall?"

After the ambulance came, after the girl was taken off to Bryn Mawr Hospital and treated for lacerations and a broken leg and dehydration, the story slowly came out. Li Fung had been reading *Jonathan Livingston Seagull*, and then decided to change her clothes. Li Fung opened her closet door, and then saw something hanging in the back. She had failed to notice that there weren't any floorboards in the back of the closet, just exposed insulation, or perhaps she did not understand that the fluffy, cloudlike material would not support the weight of her body. In any case, she had stepped onto, and then fallen through, the insulation in the back of her closet, which closed up behind her, as she fell, in slow motion, the two stories behind the walls of the Reynoldses' house. She had been knocked out, briefly, and then she came to. When she woke up, it wasn't quite clear where she was. Li Fung, in her weakened condition, had cried out softly from behind the insulation and plaster where she was wedged, but the Reynoldses had not heard her. She'd stayed like that for days and days before Mrs. Reynolds, by accident, heard the soft sounds of distress in a language she did not understand.

After she got out of the hospital, she went back to the Reynoldses as if nothing had happened, although it was true that she had bruises on her face and arms for a while, and she had to spend six weeks in a cast. The Reynoldses' friends signed their names on Li Fung's cast, but this didn't cheer her up. Before the school year began, she went back to Taiwan.

Apparently they'd gotten her out of the wall all right. But whenever she slept, Li Fung had nightmares, dreamed that she was once more trapped behind the wall of an old house, where no one could hear her voice.

One night, after the Devon Horse Show was over, after the big vans containing horses and riders and antique carriages had all driven away, my parents sat around the fireplace in their living room, talking about Li Fung.

I was playing the piano for my father. He liked it when I played the rags of Scott Joplin. My father sat there smiling and smoking as I played, his whiskey in his hand.

"Can you imagine it?" said my mother.

"Imagine what?"

"That girl at the Reynoldses'. All that time, trapped in the walls of your own house and no one even knowing that you're there?"

I played the piano for my parents in their black living room. I didn't say anything, but *Sure*, I thought. *Of course*. I could imagine exactly what that was like.

FIRST TIME

·

BY JULIE ANNE PETERS

I light the last candle
and blow out the match.
Sulfur from the smoking
tip streams up my nose as
beside me, on the edge of
her mattress, Jesi turns
and smiles. Does my
face reflect my fear?

Nicolle's scared. But I
don't want to wait anymore.

"So, um, how do we do this?"
I say. My voice quivers, the
same way my insides feel
whenever
we're this close to doing
it. "Do you know?"

"We'll figure it out."
Does she even want to?
I know it's a big step,
but we're ready. "Are
you sure, Nic?" I ask her.

"Positive."
We've been going out since
March.

March, April, May, June.
Fourteen weeks, three
days, eleven hours. If you
figure out the minutes,
the seconds, the moments,
you can express us as an
equation. 14 weeks = 70
days + 28 days + 3 days
is 101 days x 24 hours
+ 11 hours—
The time doesn't matter.
Our feelings are infinite.

She's calculating in her
head. I can always tell
because her eyes get that
faraway look and she starts
blinking real fast. She's
thinking up a hundred
reasons why we shouldn't.
She's counting down the
minutes she has left.

We were friends. We still
are, but more than that
now. Soon to be lovers. I

always thought I might
be lesbian, but once I met
Jesi I was one hundred
percent certain.

She's thinking. Processing,
processing. Come on,
Nicolle. I take her hand to
bring her back to me.

I squeeze Jesi's hand.
We had an instant
connection. We could talk.
Really talk. We talked
about wanting to be in
love, the kind of love that's
everlasting. What were
the odds? A million to one.

I raise her hand to my lips
and kiss it. I search her eyes
for doubt. Because if she
still has doubts, we should
wait. I don't want her to
ever regret this.

We laughed. That was the
thing. We laughed so easily

with each other. About stupid stuff. Suddenly the whole world was absurd.

A guy riding a bicycle stopped next to us on a street corner one Saturday and he had a Snugli strapped to his front. We were on our way to the cineplex, waiting for the light to change, and he was balancing on his bike, cooing and tickling his baby. Jesi and I glanced over at the same time and saw what was inside the Snugli. An iguana. When the light changed and they took off, Jesi met my eyes and we burst into laughter. We laughed so hard, we had to hold each other up to keep from collapsing. That was the first time we hugged.

Her eyes are twinkling,
like she's going to lose
it. If you laugh, I'll laugh
and we'll never be able
to do this.

She has this explosive
laugh that shakes her whole
body. Even when she
isn't around, her laughter
rings in my ears. Just
knowing I'll hear it every
day makes me smile.

Maybe if I start. Get her
going. I could kiss her eyes,
her lips, her neck.

Her lips are so
soft and sweet.
Over spring break a group
of us from senior senate
decided to go on this raft
trip with Outward Bound.
Jesi signed up with a club
from her school. We'd
never met, but when she

said hi to me, I felt this
hitch in my stomach.
Oh God, Jesi. When you
kiss me like that . . .

I lift her hair and kiss
the back of her neck.

The trip was four days
of white-water rafting
on the Green River and
camping on shore and
nature hikes. I silently
cheered when Jesi got
teamed in a raft with me.
The first rapid was
supposed to be easy, but
there'd been heavy
spring runoff.
The night we arrived
there was an unexpected
cloudburst, so even
though we had scoped
the rapid, by the time
we paddled to the edge
and prepped for our

run, the water level had
risen. The river raged.

She's here, then gone.
"Where are you?" I ask.
"What? Oh. The raft trip." I
turn and smile at her. "How
I saved your life."

Why is she thinking about
that now? Our raft got
sucked into a sinkhole. It
crumpled in half and I
got pitched into the river.
It was freezing. I panicked.
The force pulled me under
and I couldn't breathe.
If we got dumped, we were
supposed to keep our
feet in front of us pointing
downriver, but I was
flailing around and choking.
I felt arms around my
waist, then a push upward
toward the raft and a body
underneath me.

It was Nicolle.
Nicolle saved my life.

"I got into so much trouble
with the guide for jumping
in the river after you.
Remember that?"

"No. You did?"

"Yeah, after we knew you
were going to be okay. Then
he reamed me royally."

"Thank God you saved me.
If you hadn't, you might be
a virgin forever."
She laughs quietly. Her
foot is tapping now. "Hey,"
I say. "I love you." She's
the best friend I've ever had.
I kiss behind her ear,
under her jaw. She shivers.

I can't believe I
found Jesi, my soul mate.
We've come so far.

I trust her with my life.
"Nic," I say quietly.

"Don't be nervous."

"I'm not." I'm terrified.

I can't stand it. I lean over
and hold down her knee.
My lips press to hers, gentle
at first, then urgent. She
responds. This is going to
happen. It is.

I love to kiss her.
She's so beautiful.

She relaxes in my arms.
I comb my fingers through
her soft hair, and her
arms glide around me.

At night we'd sit around
the campfire, roast
marshmallows, and tell
ghost stories. Jesi and
I would seek each other
out to sit together,
talk quietly, or stuff
marshmallows into
each other's mouths. If
we couldn't sit together,

if we were forced to mix it
up, we'd make faces or
roll our eyes. Like, This
ghost story's lame-o.
Bloody Mary, eek! We'd
crack each other up.
Everyone wondered, I'm
sure, what was so funny.
Nothing. Life. We'd hang
out after the others
went to bed and talk. For
hours and hours just talk.
Talk and laugh.

She's off again, her eyes
glazing over. I clamp her
face between my hands.
Do you feel my crushing
need? If she thinks too
long about it, we'll lose the
moment. I want to reassure
her. I'm here, Nicolle. I'll
always be here. If we drown,
we drown together.

We weren't supposed

to wander out alone in
the wilderness, but we had
to get away from everyone.
We found a cave in the side
of the mountain. Against
the cave wall we sat in the
dark, discussing books
and movies and music and
places in the world we
wanted to go. Jesi longed
to find a place on earth
where no human had ever
set foot. Unspoiled. Like us.

I slide my hands down
her arms and she trembles
under my touch. I
know we both want this
so bad. We've been
waiting, being good,
being patient.
Waiting to be sure.

We pretended we were
the first two humans to
enter our cave.

I slip my hand under
her shirt and she inhales
a sharp breath.

Oh God, Jesi. In the cave
with our arms touching,
our natural warmth seeping
through our windbreakers.
Jesi looped her leg over mine
and I crooked my arm in
hers. She whispered in the
dark, "I've never felt this
close to anyone—ever."
I breathed, "Me neither."

My hand crawls over
her bra in front and I press
my palm to her heart.
It's beating fast.

I love her touch. I love
the feel of her skin on mine.

Her lungs fill and her
breasts expand. A shallow
breath escapes. Yes, Nicolle.
Give in to the feeling.

I breathe her in, and fly.

After that, if we weren't together, we were on our cells. I call her the moment I get up in the morning, or if she's up first she calls me.

I whisper in her ear, "I want you. I love you, Nic." She lifts her chin and I cradle her face in my hands. I close my eyes and kiss her like the first time.

Our first kiss, in her room after school. We'd sprawled on the floor and were sorting through old CDs, laughing and joking. Our heads touched and we both stopped laughing. We looked at each other and held each other's gaze. The urge to kiss was so powerful, so overwhelming.

My tongue touches
hers and I want to jam
it in her mouth. Push
her down and—
Slow. Slow down. It's
taken an eternity to get
to where we are tonight
and I don't want to screw
it up. We're in love. This
is right for us, now, at this
time in our lives.

The deep kissing
we've been doing, the
touching and stroking,
it's all been a prelude.

She lifts my T-shirt in
back. I feel both of her
hands on my bare skin and
it sizzles. We've done this
before. We've felt every part
of each other. Yes, Nicolle.
Surrender.

She makes me melt.
The way she braids my hair

in cornrows, the tingle
beginning at my scalp and
spreading all the way
down to the tips of my toes.
It's sensual anyway, when
somebody plays with your
hair, but this escalating
tension and sense of
excitement ripples
through my body.

Still! She's still processing.
Why? She drives me crazy.
From that first kiss, we
knew. God. I knew, anyway.
Our eyes lock and hold.
It's time, Nicolle. No more
longing. No more stopping
when we want to go on.

Jesi says . . . nothing,
but her eyes speak her love.
As I pull up her shirt, we
stand together by the bed.

My fingers fumble her
buttons and she tries to

help, but I nudge her away.
I want to do it. It takes me
forever. Six buttons.

Stupid, I think. Why
didn't I wear a T-shirt
like she did?

Hurry. Last button.
I ease the shirt down off
her shoulders, where
one of the buttons gets
stuck on her bra clasp.
"Shit."

A laugh lodges in my throat.

I clap a hand over her
mouth. Don't giggle.

I have to slide the shirt
back up over my shoulders
to free the button. My
shirt falls to the floor on
top of Jesi's T-shirt and
we're standing face-to-face
in our bras.

I unfasten Nicolle's bra in
front as she's undoing mine.

Hers pops open and
releases her breasts.

I gentle Jesi's bra down
her arms and off.
Her breasts are smaller than
mine, perfect. I want to . . .

My fingers graze Nicolle's
arms and it raises goose
bumps on her skin. I can't
take my eyes off her
breasts. They're, like, three
times the size of mine.
I bend down and kiss one,
then the other.

Stop. Don't stop. My
nipples are already
hard from exposure to
air, the sudden spike
in temperature, or
excitement, or anticipation.

I pinch her nipple lightly
between my thumb and
index finger.

I squeal a little,

an involuntary yip.

I do the other one.

God. I want to grab her
wrists and pull her hands
away, but the pleasure is
excruciating. Her fingertips
circle my nipples.
She lowers her head again.

I kiss her left nipple.
Then the right.

Oh my God. Torture.
Pleasure/pain. I clutch
her waist and pull her
to me. "I love you," I
expel in her hair.

"I love you too."

I hold on to her for
equilibrium. For ballast.

I breathe in and
she breathes out.

I'm so in the present
now, here in Jesi's room.
We've planned this for
weeks. I've lit all the candles.

Her spine is straight and
stiff. I run my hands up
along either side and she
arches her back.

I copy her moves.
She has taut, smooth skin.
I can feel her ribs.

We run our hands along
each other's sides and arms
and waists and hips.

My hands spread across
her bottom and she
contracts her muscles.

Nicolle's getting into it.
Unzip my jeans, I think.
Touch me there.

My hands find her breasts
and I press them up from
below. She's moist, sweaty.

She's holding up my
breasts. She's looking at
them, licking her lips.
Do it, Nicolle. Do it.

Her nipples are small

and pink and puckered.
With my hand, I guide
    one into my mouth.

                My head falls back and
                I open my mouth to gasp.

    Her fingers grip my
    arms as I nibble her.

                I try not to cry out.

        I pull back.
        "Did I hurt you?"

                "A little," I admit.

    I die. "I'm sorry."

                "No," I say. "They're just . . .
                tender. Kind of sensitive."

    "I won't touch them."

                "Yes, you will." I
                clamp her hands back
                on to my breasts.

    I meet her eyes. Even in
    candlelight—especially
    in candlelight—she has
    the deepest eyes. Honest.
    Sincere. Teasing me now.

                I widen my eyes at Nicolle

before sliding her nipples between my fingers again and squeezing.

I jump through the ceiling. Please. In your mouth. We fondle and kiss each other. The voice inside says, "Move on, move down." My right hand spreads across her stomach and over her jeans zipper and between her legs.

Oh yeah. A moan sits in my throat. I move my legs apart as my hand reaches between her legs.

I suck in a breath. I don't know how long we do this, kiss and rub each other. Groan with pleasure. We've done this before.

I'm so hot for her. I unzip my pants. Let's get to it.

Forget trying to take off

each other's jeans. We
shimmy out separately and
drop them in place.

At last we're in bed together,
naked. Well, not totally.
Nicolle kept her underwear
on, so I did too.
Under the sheet, we kiss
and hold our bodies
against each other and
intertwine our legs.

I don't know if I should
be talking to her, telling her
how much I love her and
how perfect and beautiful
she is, or just try to keep
breathing, keep my heart
beating and blood
pumping to my extremities
and lungs because I'm
panting and feeling
hammered and lightheaded.

My hand slides between her
legs and she jolts. I pull back.

"What? Don't stop."

"You're sure?"

"Yes." No stopping now.

I ease off her thong and she takes off mine. Our feet get tangled.

She kicks our underwear off the end of the bed and throws herself against me. Her hair drapes around my face like a veil. She plants kisses on my nipples and stomach, one thigh, then the other. She arcs into the air and she's over me. Her hair hides her face, so I rake my fingers through it—long, thick, black hair—and bunch it behind her. I want to see her, watch her face.

My hand slides between us, between our legs, and finds her spot. She makes a high,

squeaky sound. Her hand
is there too, on me. I take
her wrist and steer her away.
"I want to do you first."

I pause. "Don't you
want to come together?"

Yes. No. I want to tell her
I've been reading up; that
it's hard to have orgasms
together, but I don't want
to break the mood. Instead,
I simply say what I feel: "I
want it to be good for you."

It already is. What do
I do next? Just lie here? I
don't know how to do this.

The first time, I
want it to be special for
her. Memorable. It
probably won't be very
good. What if it isn't
good? She's nervous; neither
of us has ever done it.
She gazes into my eyes

and I see her desire.
It's all I need.

I cup Jesi's chin and draw
her to me; I kiss her. Her
lips are full and sweet. "Let
me do you first," I say.

"No." I whip my hair
around. "I've been
dreaming of this moment
and this is how I want
to do it."
With you. For you.

I'd been visualizing it
too. More like obsessing.
She kisses my shoulder,
my neck, my breasts.

Wait. I freeze above her.
What if . . . What if this
changes things between
us? Of course it will, but . . .
Nicolle's my best friend—
I don't want to lose that. If
we're lovers, can we still be
friends? Oh my God.

Why didn't we talk
about this? We talked
about everything *but*—

"Jesi, what?
Why did you stop?"

"I . . . you . . ." The words
clog in my throat.
She looks at me, into me.
I think—I know—Nicolle
will always be my friend.

"I'm ready."

I'm ready too.

She resumes the kissing
and I close my eyes.
Her tongue is on my
stomach, in my belly
button swirling around.
She's at my fringe.
When she spreads my legs
I'm so aroused all she
has to do is kiss me there,
flick her tongue across
me a couple of times
and I explode.

God, she's coming.

Waves and waves of ecstasy
and joy and shock pulse
through my body and swell
all my vessels and veins
and I grab Jesi's arms to
pull her up.

I dig my head into her
shoulder and press fingers
into her to keep her
orgasm coming. I feel the
throbbing. I *feel* it.

It's slowing, waning.
Too soon.

Short, concentrated bursts.
She goes, "God."
I'll never feel this close to
another human being.

I shut my eyes and open
them; release the final
spasm. "Jesi," I say to her.
"Wait'll you feel that."

"How long do I
have to wait?"

I roll over on top of her
and kiss her hard. I want to
extend the experience,
but I can't. The tip of my
tongue plays with her
nipples and she whimpers.
I kiss down her belly.
I tease the hair between her
legs until she raises
her hips and opens her legs.

It's starting.

The first feel on my tongue
is . . . gooey. The smell is
strong. Not gross, the way I
feared. It smells natural.
I want to stay and taste her
more, but . . .

"Hurry."

I drive my face hard into
her. I take her in my mouth.

I'm on the verge,
and then I can't.
My eyes squeeze tight.
Everything squeezes.

Come on.

I suck her into me
and hold on. Hold.

Breathe, I think.
Don't think. *Feel.*

She's tensing up or
something. I let her go
and she falls away.
I spread her lips down
there and lick her up
and down. Around, inside.

Yes. Like that.

My tongue, my lips,
my mouth on her.

Don't stop.

Rhythm. Steady rhythm.

Keep going. Keep going.

How long should I—
She arches.

"God, oh God."

She screams. Her hands
claw at my ears and I
scramble up on top of her,
lengthwise, my hipbone

wedging between her
legs. For pressure to
keep it going.

She rocks and grinds me
with her hipbone and I
come again. I can't stop.

"Jesi."

"Baby." I hold on to
her as if my life depends
on it. Because it does.

For a long time we
lie together, holding each
other, not speaking.

I need her. She's
my everything.

Feeling.
I don't know what she's
feeling. Rapture?
Relief? We did it. We
finally did it. The candle
flames grow dimmer
and I roll away from
Jesi to blow out the last
flicker of fire.

My eyes adjust to the
dark. I see her clearly even
in shadow. We trace
each other's faces, arms,
the curve of our waists
and hips. I want to know
the shape of her, the
smell and taste and touch
of her. I need to memorize
Nicolle so I can feel her
every night beside me,
inside me. Trust
she'll always be there.

"Jesi," I say quietly. I tell
her what I'm thinking.
"Want to do it again?"

I smile in the dark. Oh
yeah. And then she says
what I'm thinking:
"Me first." "Me first."
We both start giggling.

DEAR LANG

·

BY EMMA DONOGHUE

Dear Lang,

Happy Birthday! This one's a biggie: sixteen. Are you excited? You must be. Unless, of course, you're the kind of eye-rolling adolescent who pretends not to be excited by anything. But I doubt that, somehow.

You're probably learning to drive already: scary thought. For me, I mean, not for you. I still shudder to recall the time you rode your fire truck straight off the porch. Shrieks, hot tears springing out of your eyes, but once I brushed the gravel off, there wasn't a mark on you. I guess it's all about knowing how to fall.

You won't remember the incident, of course. Funny the way small kids are all amnesiacs. (A cousin of mine had a martini too many after her son's third birthday party and groaned to me, "All this effort, three entire years of games and songs and special moments, and he won't remember a damn bit of it!")

I thought of including a present this year, but the

problem is, Lang, I've got no idea what you like. What you're like. Do you spend all your free time online or shooting hoops or at the mall? There's this high school I cycle by on my way to work, and I stare at the clusters of teenagers outside: supermodel wannabes and geeky kids, goths and stoned-looking ones—I don't even know the current terms. I always wonder which group you'd be in. If any. I imagine you might be a loner, like I was when I was sixteen. (Well, not a sad loner like I was, writing poetry in the basement; I just mean, kind of a maverick, doing your own thing.) Unless, of course, you take after your mom, who was Miss Popularity. (Cheryl, if you're vetting this, I'm not going to say a word against you. So how about you give me a break and hand the letter to Lang, who's practically an adult now?)

When you were born, people said you were the dead spit of her, but then they always do when there's no dad. Neighbors, especially—you could tell they were desperate not to put their foot in it—they'd rush to tell her, "Oh, Cheryl, the baby's got your eyes, your chin, your coloring." I didn't see it myself. To me, your radiant moon face was like nothing I'd ever encountered.

The other day I thought of buying you a CD, an

album your mom and I listened to so much when we were waiting for you to be born that it started getting scratchy: k.d. lang's *Ingénue*. She must have told you that's who you were named for? (Unless she's completely rewritten history.) I hope you haven't found it too burdensome a name. Do people who hear it assume you're going to be Chinese, like that pianist who played at the Olympics? We thought it was more distinctive than k.d.'s others (Kathy and Dawn), anyway. We were crazy about that CD, though the first time I heard "Constant Craving" I misheard it and asked your mom what "God Save Gravy" meant; she never let me forget it. If one of us needed to make the other laugh, all we had to mutter was "God Save Gravy."

Now I've got the song stuck in my head, though I haven't heard it in years. (The Germans call that an ear worm; isn't that a great phrase?) Of course, you mightn't like it: when I was sixteen I hated any music an adult recommended, on principle. And you probably download all yours, anyway.

At the time I'm talking about, your mom was still just Cheryl, nobody's mom. Once you've been one—a mother, I mean—it's hard to remember that you were ever anything else. That's a problem with having a kid with someone, actually. It can be hard to see see each other as anything but parents; hard to remember to talk about anything but the baby. *How does Lang like the peas?* and *I found her tambourine down the back of the couch*, and *She did a huge squirty poo this morning.* (Sorry, I know that's embarrassing.) Your mom and I would sit in the kitchen having a sandwich, say, with you in your bouncy chair; we'd be talking to each other in a desultory way, but even if you were asleep we only had eyes for you. Especially if you were asleep, actually. For some reason, there's nothing in the world more riveting than a baby's sleeping face. But the point I'm trying to make, Lang, is that if you have a kid with someone you risk losing that someone. (Yeah, and maybe you'd lose them anyway, for other reasons, but a baby sure speeds things up.) I just thought I'd mention this rather depressing fact, in case at sixteen you've got any sentimental notions like I did, about how nice it would be to have a kid with someone you love.

Whoops, this letter's headed kind of sideways, sorry. But it's a bit like talking into the void, here. Like sitting in a recording studio and suspecting that the tech guys have turned the mic off and gone home. Hello, hello? Lang? You might not be reading this at all, of course.

Odds are not, in fact. But if I let myself think that way, my hand freezes up, so let's assume instead that you are reading it. I'm hoping you flick through the envelopes in the mailbox before your mom gets home; I've put LANG in big capital letters so it'll jump out at you.

Have you any idea who I am? I suppose I should have introduced myself properly, because I think your mom probably didn't show you those birthday letters I sent when you were two, three, four, five, six, seven, eight, and nine. At least, I never heard back from you. Two possibilities: Cheryl threw my letters in the trash—or she gave them to you, but you couldn't be bothered to write back to the woman who was once your YaYa. You can see why I prefer to believe the first. So every year I'd try again, hoping she'd have mellowed enough to give you the letter this time. I had a sort of ritual: The week before your birthday, I'd take a day off work and open a bottle of wine. (Have you survived a hangover yet? I didn't have my first till twenty, but your mom's first was at thirteen. Go on, ask her, see if she denies it.) When I'd finished the letter, I always mailed one copy to this old address and a second to your grandmother with a note asking her to send it on—but the woman never did care for me and my mannish clothes. (I wish you knew your other grandma—my mom, I mean. You liked her; once in her garden she let you drink from the hose and soak your clothes even though it was April.) The third copy always went into the bottom of my filing cabinet.

Glancing at the first letter now, I see it starts rather hysterically: *Happy Age Two my yum-yum from your YaYa, who misses her darling duck so much!!!* When you were a bit older I used to try to say something in the birthday letters about what had happened, in child language, or rather, the kind of patronizing, vague language adults use to children: *Sometimes it just happens that two people who love each other stop being able to live in the same house. . . .* But it never worked, so I always took it out. I'd get so angry, I'd shake. What should I have said, *Your mom, who loves you very much, thinks it's best for you never to see me again*?

I was only twenty-four when you were born: funny, that's nearer sixteen than what I am now, forty. I wasn't a complete idiot, in case you're wondering. I knew the deal: Only a handful of states were starting to allow two mothers back then, and ours wasn't one of them. If asked I would have said it was outrageous, but most days I didn't give it a thought. I had no aspirations to same-sex marriage; they didn't even use that phrase back then. When we did the pregnancy test, Cheryl and I were so exhilarated, so at one, it never crossed my mind that she'd try to take you away from me. Same thing when we filled out the birth cert the way the clinic advised us, with *Mother: Cheryl Louise Weinstein, Father: Unknown.* (If you look at your birth cert, Lang, that's my scrunched-up handwriting.) Yeah, I knew that if it came to a fight, I wouldn't have a hope in hell, but it really never occurred to me that she'd do such a thing: take you back, like a book or a ring. That's how naive I was, at twenty-four. I liked being called your YaYa; it didn't occur to me to get you to call me a mom-type name like they do nowadays, with their mummies and mommas and mama-janes, whatever. Not that it would have made any difference. I mean, I could have been called Second Chief Cherished and Equal Parent, and it wouldn't have meant squat in the eyes of the law.

I didn't see it coming, even after I moved out. I set up a nursery for you in my apartment, but then your mom started muttering about it being *too confusing for Lang.* Visits would only be *distressing,* apparently. I can forgive her those words. Even *stalker* (the time she told me to get off her doorstep or she'd call the police). The one I can't forgive is *roommate*, from that last letter she wrote (dictated by a lawyer, I could tell), informing me that I was not related to her or her child, I was just someone who used to be her roommate.

Sorry, Lang, does this sound like I'm bad-mouthing your mom? I suppose I am. But she adores you, and she was only trying to keep you for herself; parents do it all the time. The last time I wrote to you, you were only nine, and I didn't think you could begin to understand all this adult mess. (I hit a mental wall when you turned ten, I'm afraid; I did start a letter, that year, but I kept visualizing a pinched, pubescent version of your face, with a curling lip and narrowed eyes. I couldn't seem to think of anything to say that wasn't kiddy but wasn't inappropriate either.) Now you're all grown up, pretty much, I want you to hear the truth from me, or I guess I mean, my side of the story. What I dread— one of the things that's forcing me to try contacting you again after all these years—is that you might find out about me some other way. That you might decide, in that stern way teenagers think (at least that's how I thought, at sixteen), that I let you go too easily.

I swear, I kept calling till your mom got an unlisted number. I asked friends to intervene, and some wouldn't and were no longer friends of mine, and some tried and were no longer friends of your mom's. If I was a stalker, it was because she forced me to be. I hung around the library during "Books 'n' Babes," and caught a few glimpses of you through the window; at least I thought it was you, but toddlers change so fast. I lurked in parking lots, outside your daycare, in all the local playgrounds. I did go to a lawyer, but she persuaded me I hadn't a chance. (It was 1993, after all: the year a judge had just taken a toddler from a lesbian and given him to his grandmother instead.)

Another worm's stuck in my ear now: that old blues song about god bless the child that's got its own. You probably don't know it, unless there are any sixteen-year-olds who listen to Billie Holiday? I think the "it" the child's got is money, but it could be anything, really. It's a strange song, from what I can remember, because you think it's going to be sappy, but it's really pretty grim: *Mama may have* and *Papa may have*, but you're much safer having your own.

I wonder if you call him Dad? Your stepfather, I mean. At least, I presume he hung around and became your stepfather. I can't imagine anyone who met you at age one not wanting to hang around. I notice that whenever I see one of these cases in the paper (I don't look for them, but the headlines jump out at me), the birth mother has usually gotten a man, gotten religion, rejected the "lifestyle." *Christian Mother Moves to Virginia to Escape Homosexual Ex*, that's my favorite, for its B-movie wording. *Mom Wins Child from Former Lesbian Partner.* (Confusing grammar, that one.) The papers sometimes call the other woman the "nonlegal parent" or the "social mother," as if it's all about throwing cocktail parties! (God help you, Lang, if you had to rely on me to teach you the social graces.) Or the "nonbiological mother," which sounds like an ad for detergent.

Nonbiological: as if I'm made of silicon or something. A cyborg. As if I have no body, or at least not one that ever touched you, my baby Lang, ever stubbed a toe on your wooden blocks, ever got a crick in the neck with you asleep on my shoulder on the couch all night, ever registered that surge of warmth on my belly that felt like love but actually meant you'd just peed through both our clothes. I don't tell people this, because they'd think I'm making it up—not lying, exactly, just kidding myself—but I swear it's a fact: In the weeks after you were born my nipples dripped, and once I put your mouth against my left breast and you latched on for a good half a minute, till Cheryl came in and asked a little snottily what I thought I was doing. (Well, she hadn't had much sleep.) That was one of the best moments in my life: feeling your serious tug on my left nipple, seeing your earlobe working, hearing the small, intent click of your jaw. I guess motherhood can happen in unexpected ways, like a storm moving in unscheduled or a moose suddenly standing there in the headlights.

Sorry, this letter is turning out quite a downer. I'm not like this most of the time, Lang, I'm really not. Jasmine claims I'm quite fun to live with, and she should know, having woken up beside me for more than four years now. When she and I had been together about six months, an old friend of mine got drunk and told me I'd no right to still be trailing around like one of the walking wounded when I was lucky enough to have found a woman like that. So I got my shit together: I went back to college, started swimming, went on antidepressants. Most days, these days, I'm more or less okay, and that's thanks to Jasmine. She's a clown. I mean a professional one; she does the birthday-party circuit and never seems to get tired of it. I generally avoid kids, myself.

It's odd: I realize all these years I've been thinking of you as lost, but you've got no reason to think of yourself that way. It's me who lost you.

Reminds me of my cousin, the one I mentioned, with the three-year-old boy. He kept dashing off into crowds, so she got the bright idea of writing her cell number on his wrist before they went out. But the next time they were at a fair, sure enough he wandered off, and she had to have him paged three times over the course of half an hour before somebody brought him along to the Meeting Point (the booth that used to be called Lost Children till I guess they decided that was too emotive). *Why didn't you ask a lady to call the number?* she roared at him. *But I wasn't lost*, he said righteously, you *were lost*.

Fair point. For you, Lang, there's nothing missing. Nothing you're conscious of, at least. You aren't lost, you've just lost me, and you don't even know it. Though you must have wondered where your YaYa had disappeared to. *Wondered* is too intellectual for a fifteen-month-old; I mean something more primal. You must have cried for me, at least for a week or two. You must have wanted me back: riding high on my shoulders, the feel of my spikey hair when you grabbed it, the smells of me. A year and a quarter, that's not nothing. The *first* year and a quarter. Maybe sometimes even now you feel like something's missing, Lang, even if you don't know what? (Then again, who doesn't feel that?)

I once joined a support group for people who'd lost children, but I dropped out after a couple of months. (Weeks, even? The meetings made me squirm so much, I'm probably remembering it as lasting longer than it did.) The woman who ran it called herself the moderator, as if she had magical powers to make everything feel more moderate, but I just got more jealous and judgmental. On the one hand, I felt irritated by one woman who'd miscarried at four months and kept saying *my son* when the fact was—sorry and all that, but it was a fetus. The way I saw it, I'd had a real child, and she'd had a dashed hope of one, which wasn't the same thing at all. Then, on the other hand, there was this quiet Guatemalan woman, and when the moderator finally got her to open her mouth in week three, it turned out her seventeen-year-old son had been picked up by the police one night and never came home.

(They never even admitted they'd arrested him.) Hearing that woman's story made me feel like I'd no right to complain, because after all, I had no reason to fear you were suffering: I knew Cheryl would raise you well and fight your corner. Maybe I'm just not a supportive enough person to be in a support group.

I talked about you all the time, Lang, the year I lost you. I had no shame: I made my lament to any neighbor, hairdresser, grocery clerk who'd listen. (I think I must have been hoping someone would say *Why, that's just terrible. Let me start a campaign to take it to the Supreme Court.*) Then I got tired of that look of frozen pity. I didn't "move on" (as the moderator of the support group was always urging us), I just shut up.

Nowadays, people assume I'm childless. I don't blame them; if they don't know me well enough to have heard the story (and it's not one I tell at dinner parties), what else would they think? I look childless: the hair, the scarred leather jacket, the headphones, the air of having plenty of free time. Besides, moms talk about their kids, don't they? (They bore the pants off their listeners; they flash sheaves of photos like magicians saying *Pick a card, any card.*) I keep you to myself.

These days, I really only mention you to Jasmine, and not often, because it makes me maudlin. Not that she stops me. She says you're part of me, and she wouldn't want you not to be. She pictures you as this tiny invisible angel sitting on my shoulder. (My left shoulder, for some reason.)

The only big fight I remember was on our second anniversary, when she—ever so tactfully—raised the issue. *I've always wanted one*, she said.

I literally barked at her: *I've got one already, remember?* Then I left my steak untouched and I went out to sit in the car.

I know, I know. Childlessness brings out the child in me.

Something else I remember about that support group was that it gave me a warped view of the world. It seemed that the odds of holding on to a child were slim; kids were like feathers blown out of your hand no matter how you tried to clutch them. (One girl had had five in a row confiscated by Children's Aid. No, what's the word—apprehended. She never said why, but we all quietly assumed there were reasons. One week she announced to the group that she was pregnant again: She said she might be allowed to keep this one, and we all had to nod and grin as if we believed her.)

The moderator of the group was always at us to document our kids. Not as in putting together a file for the sake of proving to the newspapers that the police had indeed arrested your son. She meant a warm, fuzzy, scrapbook-type thing. A nice idea, I guess: it would make your child's life with you seem like it really happened, even if one day they'd fallen on an escalator or been snatched by their dad who took them back to Pakistan or whatever. A scrapbook like that might be some comfort on crazy days when you thought you'd imagined the whole thing. It did seem useful for the parents whose child had died, because it gave the story some shape: babyhood, toddlerdom, pony rides, trick-or-treating, hospital, funeral, with Grandma up in heaven. . . . (In a café, a friend once asked me if I ever wished you were dead so I could do my mourning and get on with my life. *Never*, I'd roared, so loudly that everybody turned around and stared. But it was true. I've always been glad you're in the world, Lang. Even if I don't know where.)

I had a scrapbook already, so I didn't do one in the group. I'd made two of them, actually; your mom laughed and said she didn't know where I found the time. LANG: YEAR ONE, I wrote on the cover of the first, like you were the start of some utopia. It wasn't a baby book like you could buy in the stores, because they all said *mom* and *dad* everywhere, obviously; it was a blank book made of bumpy handmade paper. I filled it with sketches of you and funny lists, like: date of first projectile vomiting, date first fell off sofa, first nursed for two hours twenty minutes straight, first grabbed my ears and wouldn't let go. . . . I didn't have a date for "first smile" because it seemed like you were born smiling, little flickers and twitches at least, and everybody says sternly, *Those are only gas*, and it's hard to prove which is the first real one: They all looked real to me, they just got less newborn wise and more fat-baby smart. I taped in a blackened cent you swallowed that took eight days to come out the other end.

Anyway, I don't know the actual dates of any of these milestones because I didn't think to take the YEAR ONE scrapbook when I left the house. Ask your mom if you want to see it. I doubt she's ever shown it to you, because it's full of references to me, and if she tried to cut them out it would be like one of those censored letters from World War Two, all lacy, more holes than paper.

The YEAR TWO book, luckily for me, happened to be in my backpack the night I left, because I was working on the page about your first time tobogganing. I'm looking at it now, turning the gaudy rainbow pages. It starts with your first birthday party: giant bubbles (they left sticky marks on the grass), and an Eeyore cake that you spat out because you'd never tasted sugar; it'd been all pureed yam and barley till then. As a bookmark, there's a sparkler I stuck in your cake, thinking it would be more exciting than a solitary candle, but when I held you over the table to blow the sparkler out, you grabbed it instead and burned your hand and your mom got furious with me. (She was furious with me most of the time by then.) YEAR TWO has thirteen pages filled in with things like: first concert, first entire bag of potato chips, first time you threw a Walkman over the banister. . . . (Do you know what Walkmans are, Lang? Like iPods but bulkier, and they only held one cassette. I know, seems a feeble invention, but we enjoyed them hugely.)

I don't look at it all the time or anything. A year might go by. Then I'll get into a mood to read through those thirteen pages for hours on end, and Jasmine knows not to interrupt me; she goes off and makes a casserole or something. I showed it to her once, and she read it very respectfully, holding it like it was some ancient manuscript that might fall to dust any moment. She turned over a page after a drawing of you on the sled and suddenly it was blank; she turned back to see if she'd missed something. No, I told her, it really did end on the word *mitten*.

Jesus, I miss you, Lang. Does that strike you as ludicrous? I admit I don't know the girl I'm missing. The toddler I remember from 1993 waddles and staggers, lurching through my dreams. The girl who's sixteen—her, I just have to make up in my head. For every month I lived with you, the real you has lived a year without me. Wow, you're probably a babysitter by now. (It's a great job for loners, if you are one; that's how I made my pocket money till I left home.)

What are you like? The question torments me. I know you're intelligent; that much was obvious from day one. Probably beautiful too, though it's hard to extrapolate sixteen-year-old features from the fat face of a toddler. Still quick to laugh? Once I put a wicker basket over my head and you snorted so much that apple juice ran out your snub nose. But maybe any fifteen-month-old would find that funny. Avocado's still my favorite food. Is it yours? You probably don't chase squirrels anymore, but do you still climb sand dunes? When you cross a bridge, do you stop to throw pebbles into the water like we always used to? I wonder whether I left any mark on you at all.

I've only got two pictures: the ones I happened to have in my wallet. I've blown them up to book size and framed them, but I keep them in a drawer, because otherwise, casual visitors might ask, *Who's that?* They look like two different children, though they were taken around the same time. One is a close-up of your face, but I can tell you're in the bath because of a trace of a bubble-bath goatee I used to put on you; you're showing three gleaming teeth, laughing as if you're about to go up like a firework. In the other picture you're at your birthday party, in your mom's lap, looking kind of nervous, with your shirt riding up. You're paying her no attention, but she's your safety, your springboard, your daily bread. Bitter as I am, I think I can say that I'd never have tried to wrench you out of her grasp.

I took more of the photos. (Is that the definition of a dad? An un-mom, anyway. Moms haven't got enough free hands for a camera.) There must have been pictures that showed me and you together, but I haven't got any.

There's no proof I ever kissed your velvet neck or hiked through the woods with you asleep in a carrier on my back. I don't know whether your mom threw all the photos of me away, but she'd have had to, wouldn't she? Logically.

What does she tell you when you ask, I wonder—that she was single when she went to the clinic? That you're your stepfather's, but he had a phobia about being photographed in those days? Or does she say that there was another mother, who chose to leave? She better not have told you that.

I didn't choose it, but yes, it was my fault. You're old enough to hear this, and I might as well tell you before she does. When you were a year old, Lang, I had a thing, a small fling. You're a teenager; surely you can understand acting on a stupid impulse? I was tired, ground down from arguments. I was twenty-five. I did what parents so often do, but I was stupid enough to forget that I didn't have the rights of a parent.

Jasmine always tells me to stop blaming myself; she says maybe I deserved to lose Cheryl but not you. I don't know about that, but I comfort myself with the thought that your mom would probably have cut me out anyway, sooner or later. If she always had the potential to be that ruthless, then surely the time would have come—even if I'd behaved impeccably—when she'd have fallen for some guy and told me to move out. That way I get to pretend my hands were clean.

Jasmine also says she'd love to meet you—but I can tell she doesn't believe you'll ever knock on our door. Whereas I believe it; I insist on believing it. I'm cynical enough on other matters, but on that I'm unshakable. You're my child behind a door, behind a wall, under a spell, lost in a fog. Or rather you're in dazzling sunlight and I'm in the fog. I have to believe that you'll come and find me someday—even if it's just out of curiosity or rebellion; I'm not fussy—and we'll take it from there. I don't care if you're not anything like I've imagined, not anything like me. I just want to know you.

But the wait is more than I can bear. Yesterday I saw a blond teenager in a borrowed Saturn opposite me at an intersection, and for a second I convinced myself it was you, but the eyes were wrong. I write to all the schools you might be attending, though your mom could have moved to another city, of course. (I did that myself, the year after it happened, because I couldn't seem to stop driving by the house.) I leave messages on any bulletin boards that a sixteen-year-old girl might come across; I've been kicked off a few when they think I'm a pervert.

"Why bother?" I can almost hear you asking it, in a bored voice. "It's too late now, so what's the point?" It's not even like I'm the donor: the mysterious other half of your genes. I'm just a woman who messed up her chance to raise you.

But that's not the real Lang talking, I don't believe that. That's the pouty *Gossip Girl* version I make up to scare myself when I can't sleep. I knew you for a year and a quarter, the real you; I knew you from day one. You had a generous and hilarious spirit and I'm betting you have it still.

I suppose all I really want to tell you, my daughter, is that I love you, and I won't stop. Even though—I admit this through clenched teeth—I suspect your life's been just fine without me in it. On the whole, it's for the best that you haven't known what you've been missing. And yeah, you might have been different if I'd had the chance to look after you for sixteen years instead of one, but I don't care: However you are, I don't want you to be any different.

The other reason I've gotten around to writing to you this year is to tell you some news, which I've left till the end because I don't know how you'll feel about it. Or how I feel about it, if I'm going to be honest. Did your mom and your stepfather . . . have you got any brothers or sisters? Well, you're about to get another.

I gave in, last Christmas, and not just because it wasn't fair to Jasmine. Something in me finally said yes. Maybe it was turning forty. Maybe I got sick of avoiding small children. I guess I thought I can't ever go back to being not-a-mother, so I might as well try another roll of the dice.

Jasmine got pregnant first go (so I wouldn't have time to change my mind, she jokes). He's due in November. I say he, but we don't know yet; all I know is that I'm praying for a boy, so he'll be that much less like you. But that's ridiculous, really, because babies are babies. He or she, this one will make little goatlike cries like you did, kick the air, spit up on my shirt, have little scratchy nails and a look of wonder. Some things will be different, but some will be so much the same that I could cry just thinking about it. I've decided to be YaYa again: Anything else sounds wrong.

Sixteen years is a long gap. The received wisdom's changed again: no solids till six months, crib bumpers and walkers are banned, and it's all about slings. I'll be careful this time; I won't fuck around metaphorically or literally. The laws have changed in our state, thank God, and I'll get all the paperwork done as fast as it can be. This child will get to keep his mom and his YaYa—with all our pros and cons—for life.

You can't imagine how scared I am, Lang. Not just of the usual bogies: umbilical cords wrapped around throats, SIDS, car crashes . . . Jasmine getting that mad Mussolini stare, *mine mine all mine*, and refusing to sign the adoption papers. . . . Between you and me, I'm terrified that after a decade and a half of grief and nostalgia—whining, some would call it—it's too late for me. That I'm damaged goods: that my capacity to mother is not just a little creaky but totally rusted up. That I've gotten used to my life, and I like it the way it is. That—this sounds so blasphemous, I wouldn't say it aloud—that I'll miss being childless.

Wish me luck? Wish us all luck? I hope some day you can meet this kid, Lang. In the meantime I'll raise him to look at your picture and say his sister's name.

Till next year, always,

your YaYa

THE SILK ROAD
RUNS THROUGH TUPPERNECK, N.H.

·

BY GREGORY MAGUIRE

"**C**ome here," he says.

But I don't. He is—everything—everything I want in an impossible way. The skin and silk of him, the tension of his bare foot on the sustain pedal, the shimmer of pale blazing afternoon sun in the stray hairs at the nape of his neck, the whole heat and heft of him in the third-floor rehearsal cubicle with its ancient A/C unit laboring, laboring. Shivering with effort and not cooling anything down.

The fly-gobbed window shakes in its frame, I in my ribs.

But it's not only the obvious consolation that I want. It's that other thing too. The secret of him.

"I can't hear you from over there, Roukh; the racket. This useless contraption roars like a turbine." He leans into a minor diminished chord, then strums it as a triad. "Faroukh, we got a song to finish. What are you waiting for?"

I am waiting for what I can't have. I am waiting for my voice to settle. In the next room, Abby Desroches and her partner are in the thick of their assignment. The walls are meant to be soundproof, but the toast-colored insulation panels are falling off, and besides, Abby and her lyricist have their door open because of the punishing heat.

I closed the door behind me when I came in.

"Shoot, Faroukh, we got forty minutes before they lock the gate to the pool house. What's the matter with you? Get over here."

Faroukh has left a good two hours to get through security at Minneapolis-St. Paul. It is three and a half years since 9/11, and things have calmed down a good deal, but traveling with the little ones is never easy. He's learned by ugly experience that while some jittery travelers are soothed by the sight of babies and toddlers, others can easily imagine that anyone with almond-colored skin would happily pad their children's pull-ups with Semtex in order to take out an airliner.

He's talked himself into this journey, and now talks himself through it. At one extreme, Midwesterners, so insulated in the American heartland, think of themselves as the moral as well as the geographic opposites of Middle Easterners. On the other extreme, Midwesterners cling to a preternatural sense of fairness. He'll just deal with what he finds. It's the luck of the draw.

He parks Matthias on the carry-on and hoists little Jamesy to his hip, and dials home. Gets the machine.

"Hi, sweetheart. Cleared the first hurdle, a piece of cake. The boys are docile, so they've charmed everyone. Look, I forgot to mention there's a half a bowl of chicken fessenjen behind the orange juice in the fridge—it'll be bad by Monday, so eat it up if you want. Don't forget the dog's water. I know you won't." Looks around, clears his throat. "Everyone's calm. A normal day. Haven't been dealt a single sidelong glance yet." Jamesy is starting to squirm. Faroukh concludes the way he always does from an airport pay phone but feels it in deep conflicting ways today. "I love you, honey. Always will. Whoops, there's our gate posted. Will try to use the traveling-with-young-children excuse to board early. If she's looking for them, Maman left her headache pills by the TV. Don't forget to drench the jade plant, either."

He hangs up. Actually, the gate isn't posted yet. He

can walk the boys a little and try to tire them out. In the curved steel surface of a post, he looks to himself as American as Tom Hanks. He expects to everyone else but his kids he's a dead ringer for Mohammed Atta.

In any event the boys keep busy running into the plate glass windows of the departure lounge and falling down and regaling the area with peals of bright laughter. Little terrorists.

When he settles in his seat, the airline attendant doesn't return his nod of gratitude for the extra pillows. Faroukh pulls the window shade down and tries to settle his thoughts. Every leaving is a returning, every returning a departure. Before the attendant has announced they are open for general boarding, Faroukh can close his eyes and imagine the grit gray February farmland that will scroll beneath the wings of the 10 A.M. Northwest flight, Twin Cities to Logan Airport, Boston. The hatch marks made by farm roads edging cropland. The squiggly patterns of suburban housing developments. The loose silken strand of interstate, the lazy steel of frozen river. The present crawling into the past.

From a height of nine feet—the sill of the Concord Trailways bus—I can see the occasional berm of displaced field. Diggers and bulldozers, school-bus yellow, are crawling the wrecked site. Your Tax Dollars at Work. The connector highway isn't finished yet.

I don't know I'm on my way to meet Blaise d'Anjou. Nor that the sight of this reshaping landscape will stick with me for a lifetime. I don't believe I'll have memories rich enough to last a lifetime—somehow I don't think I deserve them. At any rate, I hope any such memories don't begin and end with Laurel Finn and her broken finger. Her broken middle finger.

Though my thoughts try to trace around it, she's still there in my gut, a figment like an ulcer, an aura stained with something the opposite of charisma. I'm so ashamed. She exploded at me the night before the AP English final, charging me with all kinds of nasty behavior. First I'm disbelieving and silent, pulling my clothes back on. Then I'm begging her to shut up and calm down. Then I'm slamming the car door while she's reaching either to hold me back or to claw my eyes out. And the door catches her finger. The commotion . . . Mr. Finn in the ER waiting lounge at Phelps Community calls me a filthy Arab and tells me to stay on my side of the room; if I come within twenty feet of him he won't answer for what happens next.

I don't correct his misapprehension about Iranians being synonymous with Arabs. It isn't the appropriate moment.

Baba shows up with a plastic container of salted pistachios, which Mr. Finn drops in the nearest bin. We drive home in silence.

So I fret and I stew. I stay up all night trying to write Laurel a letter, equal parts apology and accusation and a testimony of love. Rework it, rework it. The next day, sleepless and upset, I blow the AP English final, but good. The exam on Shakespeare's sonnets, which I've loved all spring. Suddenly they make no sense at all. Neither do I. Kind Mrs. Harriet Bikovksy turns into a legalistic vulture and refuses to let me do a retake. (Has the Laurel Finn version of my shame already hit the gossip channels around greater Buffalo, New York? Is Mrs. Bikovsky doing the feminist solidarity routine? I thought she liked me.)

Since my grade point has plummeted, Colchester College sends the nicest letter revoking my partial scholarship. My only hope to salvage the situation is to take a make-up level-five English over the summer. But the local smart-asses have signed up for all the AP English; the courses are closed. Laurel Finn is going to have a lot to answer for in terms of wrecking my chance to go to college.

Then Auntie Nurjahan over in central New Hampshire happens to ring up Maman one day. They mutter in Farsi about the disaster. Auntie comes up with the idea of my spending six weeks at her place and taking a course at nearby Tupperneck College. I can earn my credits, repair my average. Auntie would love to play house with me.

Baba doesn't like Maman's sister Nurjahan, but he likes the idea of my losing the financial aid even less. My folks can't afford to send me to college without help. An immigrant at the age of twenty from the highlands west of Mashad—he and Maman left Iran in 1961 or 1962—he has seen his own hopes for instant assimilation in the Camelot era of the United States collapse like columns of ash. Prosperity isn't promised in the Bill of Rights.

They soldier on, Baba and Maman. In the little backyard of our rental flat in Tonawanda, New York, they try to grow peaches and apricots. "When we are young, we move all summer to temporary village in highlands beyond Dizbad," says Maman, her eyes bright. "Whole village goes—*Muki* leading prayers, family, grandparents, teenagers, babies, schoolteacher. Everyone walks our flocks to summer pasture, and we make religious pilgrimage. We sing. Is old Silk route. Silk Road, from China and India to markets in West." She's describing rural poverty, I know, but she remembers it as if it were the golden time. While here in rich America, everything is expensive and money for college has been tight.

The only way up and out, Baba reminds me daily since I was in fourth grade, hinges on my getting scholarship aid. School is your Silk Road, he says.

I have done okay in school. I don't possess Baba's sense of tragic separation from his homeland. So I don't buy into his panic. He insists that American college is the only way for us all to thrive: His and Maman's sacrifices, their self-imposed exile from home, will only have been worth it if I make good. It depends on me.

Besides, in some ways Baba has been more than ready for me to live far away in some grotty dorm. Out of sight, out of mind, maybe. Maybe he sees the possibility of failure in me, and doesn't want to watch it happen.

I learn over the phone that Tupperneck doesn't offer Shakespeare over the summer. Brontë sisters—that sounds wet. Puritan Literature, Anne Bradford to Jonathan Edwards? It's too Puritan at home in Tonawanda; I'm wanting to get away from perfection. Then I discover a cross-discipline course, credit given either in music or English, called Melody and Lyric: Tin Pan Alley to American Top Forty. Criticism and composition on the art of the popular song. Limited to ten music students, ten English students. They have space. I'm in. I'm no more interested in music than my peers—meaning I know and care a little bit—but lyrics are near enough poetry for me to tolerate for six weeks.

So I am shipped off on Trailways bus.

With Baba's blessings? Baba doesn't bestow blessings. He gives attitude, Persian style. "Excuse me," says Baba, "there is big difference between Summer of Love and Donna Summer. You think Baba doesn't know the musics. Baba knows the musics. Baba knows the young. You be credit to Maman and to the *jamat*, Faroukh-jan. *Behavior*. You do good grade in school so you avoid maintenance department." He works at Sisters of Charity Hospital with buckets of Lysol; we don't ask.

The bus is frigid, with an overzealous air-conditioning system. I can see though a weird sea-glass green of the windows that men on the work site are stripping off their shirts and working in streaks of sweat. Streaks of sweat down their backs. The sweat cleans the dust and that back, the one turning away, just there, is so strong: the stripes articulate the form. Draw the contours of that strength as clearly as the mown wheat field beyond shows the contours of the strong slope. The shape of America. (Hoping to be an English major, I'm guilty of standing by while my own metaphors metastasize then collapse into idiocy.)

Voices petition for my attention, distraction from the interesting views.

You are a liar, says Laurel Finn; and I feel I don't even know myself well enough to know if she's right.

You skip college, and you dig ditches, says Baba. *Or you move hospital beds around. Sisters of Charity offers many fine employments for strong, young, stupid peoples.*

You are a liar and you are cruel, says Laurel.

You say one word and your teeth are about to parade out your asshole, says her father. *Get away from my daughter.*

"Twenty-minute stop at Tupperneck," says the bus driver, pulling in at the edge of a gas station. "Potty break. If you're going on to St. Johnsbury, Vermont, or Canadian points beyond, don't wander from the bus.

I don't wait for stragglers." He lights a cigarette before pulling the handle to open the door.

What do fathers want their children to see, and why? What did Baba want for him that summer?

His habit of thinking in big, unanswerable questions hasn't abated.

The boys obediently peer out the window when, hoping to surprise them with being airborne already, Faroukh lifts the plastic shade. But they don't recognize the ground below as earth. What do they think it is? Bathwater brown, not as much snow as he'd guess. "Those are clouds," he tells them, indicating with a knuckle on the Lucite the prettier world of distant, icy domes.

They turn back to their tiny sachets of pretzels, more impressed with the in-flight dining.

"No surprise to me that Bush has creamed Kerry and won a second term," says a fellow in the next aisle. "We haven't finished kicking Iraqi butt." He turns to flick a speck from his nostril toward the aisle. His eye meets Faroukh's. The patriot has a tender, even sentimental mouth, which in almost slow motion opens and then closes before he shifts his gaze to Faroukh's children.

Faroukh leans down and says the first thing in Farsi that comes to his mind, the only thing the boys might remember from their grandfather. *"Tavalodet Mobarak."* It's a happy birthday message and means nothing today, but it works: Matthias smiles winningly. Faroukh turns back to the man across the aisle and shrugs, as if to say, *You can't win with children, can you? You'd sacrifice the whole world for them, including fellow passengers on a plane.*

At least this is what he wants to suggest. The other guy tracks Faroukh's eyes for just long enough that Faroukh guesses he is trying to memorize his face for identifying in a sheaf of enemies of the state. Were this same gaze happening before September 11, it couldn't have meant anything but sexual curiosity.

As if he realizes that, too, the armchair patriot drops his eyes and turns scarlet, busies himself with his own pretzels.

"Pierce," says the registrar, a chunky woman wearing what looks like her daughter's tank top. The stitching must be made of iron thread, the way it's able to hold in her amplitude. Her hair seems an homage to Sally Ride, or maybe that's just New Hampshire humidity.

"I'm Faroukh Rahmani," I repeat, meaning, *Not Pierce someone: Isn't it obvious?*

"You're not listening," she answers. "I'm telling you: the class meets in Pierce. Pierce 203. On the Perimeter Road, to the left as you leave the student union. Your dorm isn't listed?"

"I'm staying with a relative nearby."

"Lucky you. Class is Mondays, Wednesdays, Fridays, nine to eleven thirty, and lab Tuesdays, Wednesdays, Thursdays, four to five. Your prof will fill you in on everything else." She shakes her hair as if to liberate her mind of my tedious schedule, readying herself for the next set of questions.

"Pierce?" says Auntie Nurjahan. "I do anti-draft counseling there when is still Episcopal Student Services building."

"I didn't know you had Episcopal leanings. And I didn't know women could be drafted back then."

"I couldn't. But others could. Your Baba, for one. And then where would you be?"

I have no answer. Part Persian, part Vietnamese maybe, growing up on a rice paddy in the Mekong River delta? What possible lives have we sidestepped by the merest of accidents?

"Good of you to care," I say.

"You can't fight every enemy. You fight ones that matter. I'll drive you to school tomorrow; you'll have to walk rest of time. Is three miles. In Mashad we walk six miles every morning." Iran is always twice as wonderful and twice as impoverished as America, depending on the slant of the conversation.

"Do me good," I say, meaning it: That'll cut down her opportunities to stuff me with Persian delicacies by an extra ninety minutes a day. Mom's sister prides herself on her superior knowledge of child rearing. Being single, she has been untainted by maternal experience, which she believes keeps her idealism fresh and nutritive.

The boys have been enjoying ripping the pages out of Northwest Airlines' in-flight magazine. With deft folding, Faroukh has been supplying the boys with paper airplanes they can fly into the window, making little booming noises. It's not exactly PC, but it's better than launching them over the heads of passengers. Now the boys find the remaining pretzels and begin to squabble over what's left. Faroukh rings the bell for the attendant.

"I'm dreadfully sorry," she says, "we've closed up the galley; the pilot has rung the first bell to signal our initial descent into Boston. We'll be on the ground in twenty minutes or so. Perhaps they can wait until then?" Her deference to Faroukh as a paying customer has increased incrementally with every state they have successfully traversed without a midair calamity. Her smile of apology seems genuine. "Good little tykes. And traveling without their mommy, too."

"They're used to it."

The plane lands on time. Faroukh rings home; gets the message machine again. "So far so good. Now the hard part."

Auntie Nurjahan has been anxious about becoming stuck in traffic behind a stalled delivery truck on my first day. She can't risk being the cause of my arriving late, failing the course, losing my scholarship, and living my life at Sisters of Charity, mopping up behind my Baba. So we're twenty minutes early.

"Make us proud," she says, two hands clutched firmly on the steering wheel as if it might suddenly buck and take her away with it. Her face is thin between the cotton triangles of her flowered head scarf. "Iran brings you here, Faroukh-jan."

I've read about the campus in the promotional material. A good part of Tupperneck is made up of late-nineteenth-century cottage-style homes, purchased by the college during the Depression and modestly retooled for educational purposes. When I skulk toward my first class, I see that a city street or two must have been scraped out and replaced with lawns and walks, and the fences between properties removed. The place has the feeling of a neighborhood that has been flooded with grass.

Pierce Hall is among the nicer of the buildings, Queen Anne according to the caption under the photo. The carved front door is wide and heavy, and the slate roof slopes in several directions. Dormers and gables are finished with ornamental fretwork and shingles laid out in patterns, though the effect is diminished by having all the constituent elements painted the same dirty white. A wedding cake left in the dust. Even the field-stone porches have been painted white.

No one looks at me as I tromp into Pierce, though some pretty undergraduates at desks and file cabinets are singing out questions about the weekend to one another. The front hall leads to a wide oaken staircase in need of new varnish; the steps are scuffed almost to beach gray. I pop up two steps at a time as if I'm not a high-school student on probation, as if I have gone to Tupperneck for several semesters already. Room 203 is the main one at the top of the stairs.

Blaise d'Anjou is standing at the window, his eyes shaded, his back turned to the door. I don't know it is Blaise yet, of course. Sunlight glaring around him, I see him as a prototype for an ideal human body design, rear elevation. Such a confident carriage that for a minute I think he must be the professor, except for the shorts. He has a saucy stance but broad shoulders. College professors don't wear shorts in class. College professors don't look like—that.

Though I don't know what the *that* is.

Before I even take a seat, the professor swans in, a slender fellow who appears to be wearing eyeliner. Professor Theodore Farber. Other students clatter up the stairs. Despite the heat the professor is dry as a banana skin. "Call me *Tod*," he says, "or call me *Toodles*: Just *call* me." The class sits as if stoned. We don't know one another, but we're united in condescension.

The floors have been linoleumized, the ceilings

lowered with acoustic panels, but the walls still bloom with pale faded flowers, and the wood molding is the color of toasted honey. This was a bedroom once. An electronic keyboard is shoved against a tiled fireplace surround. I pick a seat right in the middle of the class. The immigrant's syndrome is to be more eager than Pollyanna, while the immigrant child's syndrome is to appear just perfectly eager, never too eager, for anything that's on offer around the room.

The professor goes through the syllabus. He passes around some photocopied pages. Begins to write with squeaky chalk. This is a school on a budget: He writes on a World War Two–era blackboard nearly incapable of taking any further impressions. He slips a tape into the deck and goes moony over a scratchy recording of "I Get a Kick Out of You." You can barely hear the lyrics through the static of time and the professor's breathy appreciation. "Don't expect you'll write a line worth saving this semester, not a *line*, darlings. But you'll write a thousand lines that will teach you what not to write next year, and sooner or later your ear will catch up with your heart. All you have going for you, you precious young things, is your proximity to love. All great songs yearn for love, and you know the yearning. You know it better than I do. Do I hear a demurral? No, I do not."

No one speaks a word that first morning. When Professor Farber—"No, do call me Tod, it'll improve your grade-point average"—when Tod opens the floor for discussion, no one asks a question. "Shy little pikers, you'll get used to it," says Tod, and gamely goes on to dissect lyrics of "If Love Were All," and "I Get Along Without You Very Well," and "The Man That Got Away." Outside, someone is riding a mower. You can't help thinking of the heat, and the sharp aroma of cut grass and gasoline, and wondering if the summer help has taken off his shirt because it is so hot, so hot.

"On Wednesday we'll look at the first sung line of a dozen classic love songs," says Tod. "See what is implied melodically by the shape of the initial musical statement. Cue up 'My Funny Valentine' and 'Over the Rainbow' and 'The Way You Look Tonight' and that old ditty 'I Gave My Love a Cherry.'"

Before he dismisses the class, Tod pairs us up. I'm teamed with Francesca Comstock, a black girl with a frosty manner. It turns out that one of the twenty students is missing; there are only nineteen of us. Someone didn't show. So some student has no partner. "*I'll* work with you, Monsieur d'Anjou," says Tod, "through the first assignment anyway. It's the least I can do. Perhaps on Wednesday our missing Miss Missy will show up and relieve me of the *burden*."

We lumber to our feet. I grunt an acknowledgement to Francesca, who seems less pleased about our pairing than I am. Perhaps she thinks that we minority students have been saddled with each other. On the way to the door, I see Blaise's face for the first time.

"I insist: 'Over the Rainbow' *is* a love song, only Dorothy doesn't know it yet," Tod is saying to Blaise. The professor leans forward; the student is trapped in his chair. His shoulders lurch back; his preppie olive green shirt stretches open. The whole thing constructs itself as a scene clear as a page in a pop-up book. Against his will, Blaise is a Venus flytrap, lethally attractive to any marauding honeybee. Professor Tod is a lech. Blaise's face is so shut it might as well be wrapped with yellow police procedural tape: Go no further.

It's no easier to say what makes any individual face beautiful than it is to dissect a compelling melody—and we tried all semester to name some musical attributes we could agree signified beauty. Later in my life someone told me that if you walk the sidewalks of midtown Manhattan behind the teeming lunch crowd, you can tell ninety-five times out of a hundred if someone is attractive by the shape of the back of their head. I've road-tested this theory and it holds up. Good proportions are good because they're consistent through the whole package.

Still, Blaise's face, that first glimpse of it—what is so compelling? The strength of resistance he is putting up against Tod Farber's overtures? The secret withheld? Is the racing of my heart just sympathy? Shorthand, I'd say he's an Anglo-Gallic chorister, and I confess I flatter myself by thinking, *Like my own make and model*, but presented here in a different color scheme and clearly an upgrade in the detailing. He's not quite blond, not quite chestnut, not quite perfect-looking. Just perfectly heart stopping.

I try to call out "Francesca" but I can't get my voice to work. I walk into the carved newel post at the landing and hope no one has noticed. Tod Farber's precise diction flutes out over us as we clatter around the turn in the staircase. We're all hurrying to get out, preferring the oppressive humidity outside.

Blaise is back there, incapable of doing anything

but trapping the professor. I have seen on his face that this has all happened before.

Faroukh guides the rental with a deceptively light hand, rolling his palm across the beveled rim like a young operative in an advertisement for Scotch, oiling along in a closed universe of sexy drives and sexy women. His boys are asleep, Jamesy in a car seat supplied by the rental company, Matthias tilted in a cushiony wodge made of candy-colored parkas and snow pants.

Faroukh is glad that highway driving makes the boys pass out. Neither Jamesy nor Matthias has pestered him since he pulled away from the Avis parking lot at Logan Airport several hours ago. It gives him time to remember, while they are securely caught in their own nests of dreams.

As all the young are. As he was, back at eighteen. A little more than twenty years ago. Caught in the kind of isolation and appetite that seems to be the punishment for outgrowing childhood.

The sun winks off the wheel, off his hand, off the silver band on his ring finger. Winks like a spotlight into his iris, blinding him for an eighth of a second. But no deer lunges from roadside underbrush, no kid on a motorbike swerves fatally into his lane. Everyone's safe, in that wink of an eye. Still safe. For now.

He wipes his eyes with the back of his hand. *Fatigue, all this sun on snow,* he tells himself. Again glad the kids are asleep. The little wet on his cheek would spook them. Even little kids can notice some things.

He holds the car at a steady sixty-eight miles per hour. His first approach was in a Trailways bus on some trunk road. This bypass wasn't completed yet. He keeps an eye out for the past in the shape of the hills, but of course that was July into August, 1983, and this is February 2005.

The season was different, as well as the decade.

In morning class I remain more or less taciturn, like the other straight boys. The gay boys and the girls answer the questions and argue with Tod.

Afternoons. What the course catalog called "labs" are sessions when we get together in pairs to compose in a tiny rehearsal room, one of eight or so cut out of attics in Pierce. We have assigned hours but we can vary them if a cubicle is free.

After a couple of labs I learn a bit about my partner, Francesca Comstock. Originally from Chevy Chase, she's spent her senior year at the American School in St. John's Wood in London. She's all glam-rock and the Smiths, all superior, Brit-itude, trying out some hip-hop with a put-on Rasta accent. We are chalk and cheese, as she says: Mismatched doesn't begin to cover it. Me, I'm still having Shakespeare withdrawal. Everything I write sounds like a half-baked sonnet. "Can't we make this weirdness work for us?" I ask.

She quotes a line back at me, something like "November can remember April tremblings." She says, "And this means, what? Are we talking earthquakes or masturbation?"

"I'm going to be an English major," I say. "I read Emily Dickinson and stuff."

"You need some stronger hero if this is what she inspires you to crank out."

It's hopeless. We keep at it, though. She has some talent. She just doesn't like being a team player. "I'm supposed to be learning something from *you*," she says. "You're the language guy, and this isn't language. This is shit."

"Colorful," I say.

"I'll give you *colorful*," she says. "Toodles spends all class creaming over the music of the past, but we're supposed to be learning something *now*. Can't you give me something you know now?"

What do I know now? That Auntie Nurjahan steals time at her insurance desk job doing organizing for the no-nukes movement? That Maman is seeing a doctor for headaches? That Baba has written me a postcard mentioning he has heard more talk about Laurel Finn while he endures another night of bowling with the Knights of Columbus? *My Faroukh-jan and LF?* he writes. *With all those beautiful Persian girls at* jamatkhana? *Maman says to say you one thing:* Firouza Mirshahi.

Where's the song in any of this? Where's the song in Laurel Finn? Someone could write it, not me.

"That Blaise knows what he's doing," says Francesca.

"How do you know?" Blaise hasn't said a word in class yet.

"We chatted." She looks at the piano console dubiously, switches the controls from harpsichord to strings. Noodles a jumpy little motif. "Wish I could be paired up with him."

"Who doesn't?" It just slips out, but I'm not sure if she notices. I rush on. "He's a composer anyway," I remind her. "Farber matches us up composer and lyricist for the lab partnerships."

"That's so retro," she replies. "It's so, so dance-cardy. So boy-girl-boy-girl at the school dinner."

"I never went to a school that gave a dinner," I say.

"Art is mixing it up," she drawls. "Art doesn't happen by committee."

"You want to mix it up? What if I try to write the music and you do the words?"

"How about you just sign off on the project and let me do it lonesome-cowboy-like?"

The first half of the brief semester passes. The increments by which the class begins to pull together are so slight that we hardly notice them. The trees lose the more luscious aspect of green and begin to go gray in the oppressive heat, which just won't lift. I sleep at night in my underpants, knowing Auntie Nurjahan will respect my privacy. I have to change them every morning; they're slightly crusty in the front, or still moist. I am, after all, eighteen.

Tupperneck now? As Faroukh pulls off the highway, the dropping sun on snow blinding him—what has happened to Tupperneck? Last month at the funeral Auntie Nurjahan told him: Old Tupperneck went under a decade ago, bought out for use as a satellite campus of the state university six miles away. You can hardly see where the college begins and ends anymore. Commercial development has nibbled up the last of the asparagus farms and apple orchards.

But here's the beginning of what was known as Perimeter Road, back when he was eighteen, and the old Episcopal Student Services building—what was it called, how could he have forgotten?—in which the summer had turned memorable.

Pierce. Hmmm. Of course, Pierce.

The heat continues. The Tupperneck River valley traps the muggy weather, and the damp heat makes us dawdle along the baking tarmac and the punished lawns. *Heat makes time slow down,* I think. The summer is lasting forever and it's only been three weeks.

At night, Auntie Nurjahan puts on one fan for the whole house. I lie in my sheets, twitching, caught. No breeze makes it into Auntie's sewing room, where I'm laid out among the threads and patterns, a dressmaker's dummy fallen to perdition.

The postcard from Baba has angered me. What has he heard now? What does he think I should do? What right has he got to pester me about Laurel Finn, several hundred miles away? And what need? I'm perfectly capable of pestering myself.

Laurel Finn on a warm spring night. A bottle of schnapps filched from her dad's cabinet. I like her. I do. She's quirky and kind, the only girl I know who can do imitations. (Why is it mostly men who do voices? Is it that we're the sex more used to exploiting the human capacity for facades?) Laurel can do a wicked Reagan, a decent Woody Allen. Laurel's got shortish hair and a slender figure, and doesn't dress in what passes for high-school glam. No parachute pants and green eyeliner like a lot of the graduating sexpots.

But that's what she isn't, and have I only been drawn to what she's not? The question occurs to me in the dark. I start to hum to myself to shoo away the returning waves of shame, but I can't stop myself remembering the fumbling with clothes, the realization that I needed to fake an acceleration of breathing to match her excitement. The approach, the breach, the disaster of it all. I could hardly keep from laughing nervously, trying to disguise it as a spasm of erotic enthusiasm. It was all pathetic, such a mistake, and Laurel stayed encouraging and inventive until at last she turned scornful. "Using me," she claimed. Using her? For what? "You know for what, you . . . you . . ." But even drunk she's too intact to finish the sentence.

"Are you humming in your sleep, or you want some warm milk with saffron?" calls Auntie Nurjahan through the dark. "I bring you a cup. Wait."

Warm milk in a fretful oppressive night? "Auntie, no thanks." But you don't stop Auntie when it comes to food. I shuck on an oversized T-shirt to hide myself.

Next day, when class is over and Tod is replacing his cassettes in their plastic boxes, Francesca stands and yawns with terrible venom and remarks flatly to one and all, "I just found out there's a pool beyond the Alumnae House. Most of the day it's given over to kids for a camp, but it's open to summer students from four to five. Gate closes at five but if you're in you can stay an extra half hour while they tidy up. I'm going there today."

"We have lab," I say to her.

"For all we get done at the piano, we can as easily work by the pool," she answers. Tod looks up sharply, eyes shooting from beneath his brows. He doesn't comment. I'm not sure if I'm deemed guilty by association. I make no comment about whether I'll be there or not.

I'm realizing slowly that Tupperneck must qualify

as some kind of summer camp for college kids. It has turned out that none of my classmates are locals. So none of the other Music and Lyric students have heard about this pool yet. At four o'clock a whole passel of us shows up. It's a sorry sight. The concrete is crumbling and there's precious little shade. Still, water is water and it doesn't take much to cool off.

Francesca looks like an Aphrodite of sorts. Her black skin gleams in the water, set off with cosmopolitan glamour by the white one-piece with a bare back. She swims for a few moments, and then arranges her towel on a ledge. I have plunged in the water and I stay there near her, like an adoring acolyte, though I'm immersed out of a certain sort of modesty if nothing else. I know I have a pair of swimming trunks in my duffel bag at Auntie's house, but I haven't wanted to walk there and back in the worst of the afternoon heat. Instead I've bought a pair of Tupperneck boxers from the campus store. They have a slit fly but I keep my briefs on underneath for safety's sake in case the fly waffles open when I walk.

I'm at chin level, therefore, trying to work the conversation around to our project—trying to be heard over the flamingo squeals of the Gay Boys' club—something about water and near nudity has released their latent hysteria—when Blaise shows up. I see him coming through the gate, looking left and right, assessing the arrangement of familiar people around the pool, and selecting a chaise lounge as algebraically far away from the greatest number of us as it is possible to be.

"Yo, Blaise," calls Francesca languidly, not letting him get away with it.

He raises his hand to signal he's heard her, but keeps walking. He wears an oversized white T-shirt, and as he turns into the wind—a lovely, useful wind, the first and maybe only wind of the season—his shirt luffs up for a moment, revealing a glimpse of turquoise Speedos. No one notices that I'm staring, because everyone else's eyes are also trained on that spot of color, a concentrated essence of Mediterranean sun on a blue-green sea. It startles me, I admit—not just the look of him, so attractive, so possessed, but that he who is so retiring would come to the pool in a suit so revealing.

Then he sits down and pulls his oversized shirt down to his upper thighs, and hauls out a book. I plunge underwater to be alone for an instant, alone with the picture in my mind of one curve of flesh sheathed in emerald blue.

We wait, we talk, we chatter, we pretend to work. Some swim. The gate is closed; other students who have raced in the sweltering heat from classes let out at 4:50 are turned away. "Fifteen minutes," calls the lifeguard. I bet she too is hoping for a glimpse of our very own Greg Louganis in his peacock briefs. "Last chance for a swim."

"Hey, Blaise," calls Francesca, rising from her towel in her white-and-black glory, "ain't you hot over there? You look hot. Come on in for some laps."

He puts his hand to his eyes as if he hasn't noticed anyone else at the pool. "Sure," he says, and tosses his book aside. It feels as if the whole town is holding its breath. Abby Desroches begins to sing the chorus from Hall and Oates's "Maneater." For a second I think the gay boys, who burst into song at the slightest provocation, are going to chime in, but they're too busy holding their own abs tight while Blaise passes. He reaches the pool's edge and dives in. All any of us get is the merest glimpse of his iridescent behind, because he hasn't shucked off his T-shirt. He swims in a T-shirt the size of a canvas sail. Figures.

Francesca dives after him with a flick of her own pink insteps, dismissing me good and proper. Well, if she can get Blaise's attention she's welcome to it. I don't want to appear a voyeur. I leave the pool. No need to call my good-byes to anyone. No one is paying attention. I head for the locker room.

I'm half into my clothes when it occurs to me: I could have had a shower. I could be in the showers right now. Maybe he's the kind of guy who likes to shower after a swim. If I'm there first it won't look like I'm tracking him. Actually I shirk from showering in public, and in the high-school gym class I avoided it. The coach beat up on me until I told him it was against my religion. He couldn't verify this one way or the other and he let it go with "Furriners."

I'm shy about my body, even shyer about other people's bodies, and I'm not easy being naked, but I grab a towel and hit the shower. I spend twenty lonely minutes getting myself as clean as I've ever been in my life. By the time I give up and turn the water off, the lifeguard in the hall is reaching her hand in the men's locker room door, switching the lights on and off to hurry me up. "You're the last one," she brays. "What do you need a shower for after a swim?"

"Get the chlorine out of my hair," I call back. She turns the lights out for good. I'm in a darkening, mildewy, empty locker room. Polar opposite of erotic. I kick the metal door closed so hard it bounces back and catches me in the knee. A small bite of blood. *I deserve that,* I think. And walk home.

Faroukh finds a parking lot on the campus, but it's not half full. He must be early yet. The boys stir softly as the car slows.

He guides the car around the campus road. Some trees are gone. Some lawns have been filled in as parking lots. But in winter everything looks sparer. In the summer the big old maple behind Pierce made a green screen against anyone looking over from the third floor of Cabot next door. You could be next to naked in the back rehearsal room and no one would know. Unless someone had climbed up into the tree, of course.

He's come all this way, and now Faroukh doesn't think he can look up at that particular window. But he makes himself glance as the car turns, catches a portion of eave and roofline. There it is. No air-conditioning unit in it now. A shade. Pulled down. Is it still a rehearsal room? But Tupperneck is gone, the Episcopal Student Center is gone. What does the sign hammered onto the front porch say? He swivels his head. STUDENT ARCHIVES. Pierce is probably a warehouse, its attic a place where old transcripts are stored. Entrance essays. Copies of senior theses. Yearbooks, maybe. One year shoved on top of the other, pressing themselves flat. The spice of a thousand lives, their reek, their innocent hopes, their unspoken dreads, reduced to paper and dust.

One day Francesca explodes at Professor Tod Farber. "Everything for you is, like, a love song," she says. "'Baby Beluga' is a love song. 'Officer Krupke' is a love song. 'America the Beautiful' is a freakin' love song. 'Happy Birthday' is a love song."

"Ah-ha," he says, pointing a too-manicured finger at her. "I never said *that*. You said it, Miss Comstock. You're on to something important. So what does that mean?"

"It means you're not getting enough," she snaps. The class snorts and Tod Farber pulls himself up. His right hand smoothes the flowery black rayon of his sleek Montreal-style shirt, which is tucked ultraneatly into the top of his black cotton dress shorts. He's always crisp and cool as a folded napkin on a table set for a formal goth dinner.

The class goes quiet. The heavy boy in the back, the indie-rock bottle blondes with phosphorescent plastic skeletons hanging from their ears, Blaise in the sultry coat of silence he wears like a penance. Abby Desroches, the minimalist from Vassar. The gay boys, all puppyish and fawning in the front row. No one likes Professor Farber. No one wants to see him trashed to his face, though.

"I was about to say, Keep the personal out of it," he remarks at last. "But that would be against my code of pedagogy. Put the personal in it and you just might get somewhere, Miss Francesca. So why don't you and your writing partner do me up thirty-two bars on the topic of someone you know 'not getting enough,' as you so directly state it. Ballad, anthem, patter, verse and chorus, your call."

"Fuck you, Mr. Farber," says Francesca.

"I gather that would solve the romantic problem you ascribe to me," he replies acidly, though his expression turns sweeter by the moment, "but your remark doesn't count as completion of the assignment. Leave the lyric to Faroukh Rahmani. Have it on my desk next week."

He plunges from the room. The class still has twenty minutes to go, so no one is sure what to do next. The gay boys whisper. The big kid raps out a rhythm on the desktop.

"This is just so much bull," says Francesca. "There must be some local mini-mart where we can buy ourselves better college credits than these?" She slams out of the room. I swivel to watch her go, which allows me legitimately to turn toward Blaise. He is hunched forward over his desktop, abstracted and serene as usual. His winter-wheat hair falls down over his forehead.

I don't know if he sees me staring at him, or if anyone else does. When he glances up toward the door, his gaze sweeps past me without registering me. I turn, thinking it might be Francesca come back, or Mr. Farber maybe. Standing at the door is Laurel Finn. A small suitcase on wheels. She looks pale and gluey from hauling it up the steps.

Faroukh keeps the car slowly rolling. He isn't ready to submit to the necessary moment; but Matthias is stretching, and true to form, he begins to pinch Jamesy to wake him up too. "Don't, Matthias, please," says Faroukh.

"Are we there yet?" says Matthias. Jamesy begins to wail.

"Give this to him," says Faroukh, passing back a

sippy cup he's had at the ready for some time.

"I want to go home," says Matthias.

"I didn't say throw it at him. You said you'd be good, Matthias."

"I *was* good." While he was sleeping Matthias was good. Fair enough.

Faroukh doesn't believe in bribing kids with food, especially not kids from Hispanic backgrounds. He has read too much about juvenile diabetes afflicting Central American kids who scarf down the junk diet prevalent in the States. Still, today is a challenge; first things first. He steers the car back onto Perimeter Road. There's still a half hour. He'll go into the center of town, find a place to change Jamesy, freshen them all up. Nothing brings you down to earth like a baby's diapers.

"Jamesy's dropping his goldfish in the cigarette thing and there's cigarette things in there."

Did 007 ever get married and have kids? How did he keep from slaughtering them with some cunning mechanical device left over from his salad days?

Not for the first time this trip, Faroukh thinks of his own father. He wishes he could say, *I get it, Baba. I get it.* But it's too late for that now.

"Jamesy's eating the cigarette things."

I can't bring myself to speak. Instead it is Abby Desroches who says, "You looking for Professor Farber? He left."

"Faroukh?" says Laurel.

"What are you doing here?"

Do I really bark my greeting so rudely? I've apparently given a cue for everyone to pack up their books. Farber's not coming back and Francesca's not coming back. The next scene is starting and they're not in it.

"It's a free country," says Laurel.

"Whoa, comin' through," says the fat boy. He hears the cudgel in her simple words and wants no part of this. Laurel moves aside so he can get past.

I'm thinking, *shit*, I'm thinking, *stalker*, I'm thinking, *revenge visit*. I'm thinking, *no way*. "Want to get a soda over at the student union?"

She neither nods nor objects but darts a sideways glance at Blaise, who is standing up. "Are you feeling all right?" he says. It's the first time he's addressed anyone in three weeks. And he's talking to *Laurel Finn*. Is this my life? I feel as if I'm going to pass out.

"I'm a bit peaky," she says. "I walked from the gas station but I took a wrong turn by the Rexall and had to backtrack."

"How'd you know how to find me?" I ask. Though who cares: She's found me.

"Sit down, anyway," says Blaise, looking at me as if I'm a cretin. We're the only ones left in the classroom now. The gay boys are twittering as they dance down the stairwell. They're all agog over Blaise of course, but at least they have one another to whisper with.

I don't want to talk to Blaise, I don't want to introduce them, I don't want any part of this. "This is Laurel Finn," I say. The phrase *a friend of mine* comes up, but I can't say it. I don't think it's true anymore.

"Right," he says, and shoulders his knapsack. "Keep out of the sun."

This is as close to being alone as Blaise and I have ever been. If he leaves? Laurel will turn cryptic and weird on me. "We're going to get a soda," I say. "Want to come?" My desperation is blatant enough to blister the wallpaper and steam the windows.

He pauses. "I was supposed to work with Professor Farber after this session. But I don't know if he's left campus or what. I guess I better go to the rehearsal room." He nods to Laurel. "Nice meeting you," he says, and to me—the tiniest half glance, as if he's never noticed me before in the class, and I believe he never has—"Another time, maybe."

His calves pistoning, his backpack thwacking on those shoulders, his hair sheafing. He disappears down the stairs. *Another time. Maybe.*

I'm safe because I have a girlfriend. He can talk to me because I have a girlfriend. I'm not a threat like Professor Tod Farber or the gay boys or who knows else. You look like Blaise d'Anjou, you have a name like a celebrity chevalier out of *La Chanson de'Roland*, and the whole world is hitting on you, wanting to chummy up. Wanting to curry favor. Wanting you to look at them.

I could almost be glad of Laurel Finn, for a moment. When might *another time* happen?

"I'm pregnant," says Laurel.

I look her in the eye. I say, "How's your finger?"

The village of Tupperneck has changed more than the campus. They've rerouted the main street and put in a sad little city park. The snow has a charcoal crust. Faroukh negotiates an angled parking spot and locates a fast-food joint.

He changes Jamesy. He orders a coffee and two chocolate milks and then, surrendering to expediency, adds two packets of fries. He knows the boys will eat less than half a packet and spill the rest on the floor. But it buys him a little more time. The event starts in twenty minutes. He doesn't want to be the first one there. He wants to lurk in the back. In the shadows, as much as he can. As much as Jamesy and Matthias will let him.

He loves them so. With their little clumsy fingers doing sword fights with the French fries. The sweet clammy smell of little boys. The sweet clammy smell of family. "Not in your hair, Jamesy. Matthias, not in your hair either."

"It's blood."

"It's ketchup and don't waste it."

Don't waste your own breath, he tells himself. When did boys ever listen to their dads?

I walk downstairs with Laurel, back to the porch. Since Blaise has gone, the other students have disappeared too. The campus wilts as if the sun were storming it from every angle at once. I take care not to guide Laurel by the elbow. I hold the door open for her, that's all. I'd do the same for Auntie Nurjahan. I'd do it for Francesca or for Professor Farber, for that matter. It doesn't mean anything.

The student union is nearly deserted because it's a

Friday; everyone who can manage it flees for the weekend after morning classes. A woman with some sort of learning disability pushes a broom into the wall and leaves the dirt in a line by the baseboard. There isn't even a cashier so I drop a dollar fifty on the register and we help ourselves to drinks. I get a Coke, Laurel a glass of milk. Though there are booths to one side, I steer Laurel to a table right in the middle of the room. I have nothing to hide.

After her first sip, she says, "You ran away."

"I flunked my AP English final. You probably heard."

She shrugs, as if I must have schemed to flunk my English final so I could have an excuse to leave town. "Are you coming back?"

"If I pass this course and get my financial aid restored, I'll be at Colchester in September. Like I planned."

"I mean are you coming back to Tonawanda between now and September? When this little charade is done?"

A *little charade* just about covers it, but I don't want Laurel to know that. "I'm not sure." And I'm not. I haven't thought that far ahead yet.

"Milk sometimes makes me throw up," she says, taking a big sip. "I never can tell."

"We'll know soon enough."

Like a fourth grader, she sips some liquid up into the straw and then moves her finger over onto the top of it. She lifts the straw so its bottom is three inches above the rim of the glass. A white drop forms on the tip, defying the tension of suction, and she lets it fall onto the tabletop.

"I'm pregnant."

"So you said."

"I'm sure about it too."

"Clarity's useful. Why are you telling me about it? Do you want congratulations?"

"You know why I'm telling you about it."

"I'm not even going to talk to you about it if you begin to suggest anything."

"Who's suggesting anything? Got something on your mind, do you?"

"I think *I'm* going to throw up. Laurel, I'm not going into this. Glad you came, hope you liked the bus ride, don't know what you're doing tonight but I'm busy. This has nothing to do with me. I'm not going to spend one moment letting you pretend to us both that it does."

"I talked to your father," she says. "I had to convince him not to come up here. He says it will give your mother a headache so big she will die, so you better not tell her."

I govern myself. "So how's old Baba? Keeping well?"

"You didn't used to be so mean." Her eyes fill up. "When did all this happen?"

"People use each other all the time," I say. "I take responsibility for what I did, Laurel. I'm not answering for what I didn't do. Either you're faking a pregnancy or you've been seeing someone else. You know it wasn't me. You know it couldn't be me. And stop doing that thing with the straw, it's creepy."

"Is he your boyfriend? That kid in the class you invited to join us?"

I pretend I don't hear that. "Or putting the best spin on it, you're simply mistaken. I hear the tests can be wrong, you know. Did you do it twice?"

"Did I 'do it'? Twice?"

We leave it at that. Leave the milk and the soda. Walk in the heat. She has already arranged to stay at Auntie Nurjahan's.

"Stay as long as you like," I say. "Move in. You can

take my place in the family, and be Baba's new ticket to American life. I'll find digs somewhere around here."

"Should I worry about, you know?" she says.

"'You know?'"

"The virus. The gay virus. They say straight people can catch it."

"You can worry about whatever you want. I don't think being gay is any more contagious than being straight."

Which is the most awful thing I have ever said in my life up to then, because I know what she means. But I won't give her the dignity of letting her words sound possible. Not a single syllable of them.

"In a song," says Professor Farber, "every word has to be true. Every note. One false step, it collapses. A song is too brief to get it wrong." He smiles wryly at the ceiling, as if he wants to add, *And so is life.* But then we get life wrong all the time, don't we? And it's still life.

Left to myself, I head back to Pierce.

The boys are sensationally pleased, sparky and full of themselves. A little starch, a little attention, that's all it takes. A little staying in one place. It works miracles. The fluorescent lights give Faroukh a headache, but he relaxes here. Nothing like the safe anonymity of a plastic booth cranked out of some factory and shipped the same to all forty-eight contiguous states. The ordinariness of it, the security of it. The color of it. Carmine red, a fake, glazed color, that does nothing for the appetite and less for the ego of the adult, but shows up the beautiful boys who are standing on the bench, leaning against the tabletop, grinning their gummy smiles at their incidental dad, creasing their cinnamon-roll cheeks and chins at him.

And here is Tod Farber, barreling up the steps of Pierce at 7 P.M. on a Friday evening. He's sporting a waist-length dark charcoal jacket, cut snug at the hip and becomingly broad in the padded shoulders. So trendy that I become suspicious. "Why, it's none other than our young Faroukh Rahmani," he says. "I haven't seen you burning the midnight oil here before. Are you working overtime with Miss Comstock on that little ditty I assigned?"

"Francesca's remark had nothing to do with me," I say. "I don't know why I should get saddled with a punishment assignment."

"Roll with the punches, my boy. Being in the business means doing the work that's thrown your way. Call it the cost of collaboration." His cheer is unctuous. "She's talented, you know, behind that posturing. And she knows it. She might be the one among you to make it. There's always got to be someone."

"And I'm chopped liver?" I can't help myself. Through no fault of his own, Professor Farber is getting the backlash of my irritation at Laurel.

"You," he replies, "as I remember, are a Shakespeare sonneteer gone south. Not that I mind. You'll find something to contribute here, or something to remember later. Everything is useful if you figure out how. Where's Francesca, then?"

"I haven't seen her since class. We made no plans to get together tonight."

"Is that so." He is carefully working a set of keys out of his tight trousers so as not to stretch the fabric. "You're doing some wordsmith business here alone, then? Why not at the dorm? Too noisy?"

"I don't have a dorm room. I don't have a place tonight. I'm sort of exiled from my aunt's house."

"I see." I have caught him in midstride, though I

haven't meant to, really. "Footloose and fancy free, are we?"

"Not that free."

At least he laughs. "Surely you don't charge?"

But this is too glib; I'm being whirled out of my depth by this grown-up game of double entendre. I can't compete; I'm too lost, too earnest: I know that about myself. It's what pulled the wool over Laurel's eyes about my friendship with her. Over my own eyes too.

"I don't have a place to stay," I say at last. "I was hanging out here hoping someone would show up."

"Someone," he says lightly. "Which someone?"

I don't have the answer on my tongue. Not for him.

"I'll give a ring to one of your chums in the class, if you like," he says. "When I get to my office. Anyone special?"

He's wanting me to say it and I won't. I can't. I shrug.

"Come up?" he asks. I shake my head. "I'll call down then if I rouse someone for you."

Ten minutes later he trills, "Herbie says you can flatten out on his floor. He has a sleeping bag. He's in

Coolidge 317. The door will be propped open with a bike pump."

"Thanks." I mean it as much as I can. Herbie is the fat guy. Nice enough. Clearly a good soul. Not Blaise.

And I'm halfway across campus before I think: *So what* is *Professor Farber doing in Pierce at that hour? All dolled up like that? He's still collaborating with Blaise d'Anjou. Maybe they're working together in one of the rehearsal rooms.*

I remember the maple tree. How hard could it be to scale?

Not hard at all, it turns out. And even though the windows are black, I climb the branches slowly, hoping campus security doesn't train spotlights on me. How would I explain this to Tod Farber? To anyone?

I get up to a good height and peer in all the windows I can. I don't know what I want to see. The professor attacking the student with lust. The student beating the professor back. The student succumbing with eagerness. I don't know.

I want to see myself in that room, that's what I want. But the rectangle above the air-conditioner is black. If Blaise is in there, I can't see him. I can't see anything except a faint reflection of myself among maple leaves, like a ghost from the future, peering back at my feeble unorganized life during the summer between high school and college.

And now it's time to go.

The kids allow themselves to be slung back in the car. They giggle at the curves, rolling into each other as best they can given the seat belts. They don't swipe at each other, or taunt. Perfect children, these few moments when no one is watching them.

This time, coming from the other direction, Faroukh sees the sign at the edge of the satellite state university campus. Now the place is called the Tupperneck Arts Division. Plastic letters on a portable sidewalk marquee announce tonight's event.

Herbie's cool. I tell him more about Laurel than I expect to. The misunderstood cues, the sudden lunges, the feints toward normalcy, the aborted seduction. The shame, the misery on both sides, the loss of face. And then Laurel's impossible accusation. Impossible. On top of her broken finger.

"What if she did it with someone else and is going

to name you as the father, though?" says Herbie. "Sheesh."

"It's a total non-event," I reply. "Chill out. She's not in the club yet."

"Maybe she is now. Maybe you pushed her toward someone with more, um, oomph."

"Maybe you should go soak your head, okay?"

Herbie says conversationally, "Maybe. Don't jump down my throat."

"No worry about that."

He laughs. "I'm not worried. I could roll over you and squash you silly. Anyway, you're not into that and neither am I."

I say, with a relief I try to disguise, "What're you into, then?"

Herbie closes his eyes. "Depeche Mode. Depeche Mode and the Deller Consort. The Grosse Fugue. And Laura Nyro, the early stuff. And extra-crispy KFC. And some pot when I can get my hands on it. You?"

Me? I'm into Keats, and Shakespeare when I can understand him, and Emily Dickinson. Them, and Blaise d'Anjou. His shoulders. His waist. His calves. His thighs. His muscled— Well, his style.

Not his eyes, though, for who has seen his eyes? He

doesn't give a glance away for love nor money.

Have I telepathically infected the silence? Out of nowhere, Herbie says, "So what do you think is the big deal with that Blaise guy?"

"Big deal?"

"You know. He's so—secretive. Aloof. Thinks he's better than the rest of us?"

I know better than to begin to defend him. "Beats me."

Herbie rolls over and almost at once starts to snore, as I imagine a manatee might, if manatees snore. I climb into the sleeping bag. In this dorm room I feel arbitrary, overlooked, and welcome, all at once.

Now the parking lot is filling up. A traffic boy waves a red baton to signal Faroukh a space, but Faroukh deviates toward the small lot behind the old library—in case he wants to leave as soon as he gets there. No incoming traffic to deal with.

There will be incoming traffic, it's clear.

Is that Abby Desroches getting out of the blue SUV?

Next morning I ring Auntie Nurjahan at her job. "Is she still here?" I ask.

"Your friend, you mean," says Auntie Nurjahan dryly.

"I'm referring to Laurel Finn, a girl I used to know from high school. Last month." My formality is meant to be abrasive, and it works.

"She is here," admits Auntie Nurjahan. "Later today I put her on bus home. One P.M. I hear more than I want to hear. But Faroukh-jan, I still am not believing she has baby inside. No matter what she says."

"She can be pregnant if she wants. She can be—it doesn't matter. Whatever she wants. It has nothing to do with me."

"I believe you." But I'm offended that Auntie Nurjahan even thinks she has to defend me. I'm her *nephew*. Laurel Finn is just some troubled girl who has invited herself across state lines hunting for me. Breaking into my life without my invitation.

"She is gone by time I get home from work," says Auntie. "I make beautiful khoresht last night and still is plenty. Also fresh yogurt from scratch, very very nice."

"I have to study for the midterm exam." I'm punishing my aunt for any slight thing she has ever done wrong.

"You can study at home . . . Faroukh-jan?"

But Auntie Nurjahan's doesn't seem like home now.

Around three o'clock I turn up for a change of clothes, and I lift forty bucks from my aunt's cash stash hidden under the plastic silverware tray in the drawer. I leave an IOU under the tray and a note on the fridge: WORKING HARD. GONNA ACE THIS ONE, INSHALLAH. STAYING ON CAMPUS F. Intentionally vague about my whereabouts. Herbie is being easy-going. I think he imagines me as a kind of liberated parakeet who shows up on his windowsill. He feeds me crumbs and doesn't scare me away. That's enough, for the time being.

Wednesday the great heat inversion is cut for a day by a mass of thunderheads moving through the region. They circle about leaving huge wakes of rain. Everyone is drenched by the time they get to Pierce 203. I twist at the door, trying to shake off my curls. Blaise is a few feet away, slicking water off his front, pressing his hands against his Oxford shirt. He doesn't have a T-shirt on underneath; I can tell by his nipples standing up against the yellow cotton when his hands press against his abs. A different wetness rises on either side of my mouth, bathing either side of my tongue. "Damp outside," I say, glamorously stupid.

"Damp inside." Oh, what a pair we are, the repartee.

In waltzes Tod Farber, dry as a peacock feather. He hands out the midterm and we settle down to it. The essay questions are equally divided between lyrics and music: English students have to answer one melody question and three lyric questions, and music students vice versa. I select a music question first, because while I used to play the piano a little and know some basic music theory, it's not my strong suit and I want to get it out of the way.

Select a popular song from the list below, or nominate your own selection, and discuss whether and how the melody (and accompaniment if pertinent) makes the argument that the lyric makes. Speak to tempo, meter, modality, key, length of line, use of motif and variation, repetition, and overarching shape.

The list includes ten songs whose lyrics we've discussed in class. I settle on "Can't Take My Eyes Off of You." I write about how the melody starts on the fifth, halfway between the octaves of the tonic, which is a breathy place to start, and can move in either direction. Will it be a torch song from here, or a rhapsody with a hope for a big emotional payoff? Then the melody drifts down toward the tonic in phrases gnarled and tight, the intervals no broader than a whole note. Like someone dancing on a single square of linoleum, but still dancing.

I go on like this for some time, feel I'm on my game. I like the song better once I have written about it. By comparison, the three questions about lyrics seem like three pieces of cake. I'm the first to hand in the paper.

"You're not dismissed yet," says Tod. "Hang out through the rest of the session till all the papers are in, will you, dear boy?"

I watch the rain on the window, and tap my fingers on my forearm. It's the melody I've just written about. *You're just too good to be true. Can't take my eyes off of you. You'd be like Heaven to touch. I want to hold you so much.* I imagine that Blaise d'Anjou is watching my fingers on my arm and decoding my message for him.

"Time up. Papers in," says Tod. People groan and scrawl final lines. Abby Desroches grabs her long bushy hair in a fist and pulls it hard, biting her lip. One of the gay boys collects the papers. I guess it's David Goldstone. I guess I can give them names by midterm. They don't threaten Blaise. They don't threaten me.

"As you've noticed," drawls Tod, "our friend Francesca Comstock hasn't shown up for the midterm. She's withdrawn and we shall not see her likes again in the next three weeks. One hopes."

No one gives Professor Farber any quarter. Even now. He has a way of turning every moment into an opportunity for self-mocking. "I'm going to shake things up a little for the second half of the course. Break up your cozy little partnerships and let you try working with someone else."

We protest. Most of us have only begun to learn the real possibilities of collaboration. We don't want to shift now.

Tod listens and plays Professor Big Heart. "You're a feisty bunch. All right, then. I'm not unreasonable. We'll stay the ship of state on her course. You've asked for it, you've got it. I'll keep working with Monsieur d'Anjou, and—"

"Sir." Blaise raises his hand. That's so grade school; no one raises a hand in a college course. "Perhaps I should work with Faroukh, since he's without a partner now."

Farber is standing up at his desk. His hands grip the test papers, and one by one he straightens them with compulsive exactitude. The pause is long enough so that everyone feels it. No one moves. "You have saved me from myself," says Farber at last. "I had hardly noticed Ms. Comstock's absence, I mean not in this *context*. Your suggestion makes perfect sense. You'll have to make up for lost time, but no doubt you're up to the task. Very well."

Everyone shambles to their feet. No one wants to stay; no one wants to go out in the rain. Farber snaps his briefcase closed with a flick of his wrists. Then we stand and mull and look anywhere but at each other, Blaise and I, as the other students hunch themselves into windbreakers and hooded sweatshirts marked TUPPERNECK.

We are at the top of the stairs, heading down. He is a little broader, a little taller than I, but not much—an inch or two. Our shoulders bump and I recoil so fiercely it's amazing I don't topple into the stairwell. "What're you working on, then?" he says. "What topic have we got?"

"I don't know," I manage to say.

"So far I've been responding to lyrics instead of the other way around. You want to work the same way? Farber's come up with some pretty pasty stuff. Eurofaggy soupy stuff like the rest of that crowd."

"I'll work any way you want."

"Let's grab some lunch at the union and see. You have the work you were sharing with Francesca?"

I try to listen to his suggestions on how our collaboration might work, though I can barely hear him through the music of blood pounding in my ears. We reach the student union, dripping wet. Standing together in line. A pair. It seems as if I can smell laundry soap all over him, into his socks, between his toes, under his arms, in the warm folds behind his knees, when we sit down together and he curls one leg around the other. It's a defensive position: I know it. It would take a crowbar to unhitch one ankle from the other. A stick of dynamite to unclench those legs.

"She wanted angry," I say. "She hated the ballad stuff. She was trying to get me to pull some useful rage. I told her I didn't have access to the amount of rage she had. She said I wasn't trying hard enough."

"She was probably right. Can I see it?"

I pass over a page. Thank you, Francesca, for demanding something other than a dewy love song. "Don't read it aloud."

He starts to read it aloud.

"Mergers and acquisitions
Perjuries and inquisitions
Injuries and suspicions
Who were you with last night? Don't lie.
Hostile takeover
I'll give you a run for your money.
Don't move a muscle, you. Don't even try."

It goes on like this, I'm sorry to say. He finishes and puts the paper on the table between us. "A lot more ballsy than I'd expected. You seem so mild."

"I do?" The stupidest, mildest thing I could possibly say.

"I'd been expecting something nostalgic about the highlands of Iran or something. This is very Wall Street. Proto-Americana. I wouldn't have guessed you'd be up on bull markets, Reaganomics, all this current trickle-down stuff."

Even the words *trickle-down* make me squirm. I can't eat the sandwich I bought. "How do you even know I'm Iranian?"

"Good guess."

I raise my eyebrows.

"We have Iranian friends in France," he admits. "Teheran financial guru types who escaped with their buckets of cash during the revolution, four years ago. You sort of fit with them—an American version, I mean."

We Rahmanis weren't the buckets-of-cash type of immigrant, but I'm impressed. "Well, what do you think of the draft?"

"This isn't anything like what I thought I'd be working on, but I can give it a shot. Want to meet me this afternoon?"

"You want me there? Francesca wanted me far away. Preferably Tokyo."

"Sometimes a weak lyric line has to be reworked to respond to a strong melodic rhythm, don't you think? We're supposed to be working together."

"Guess so. Sure, today's fine."

I want to ask him: Why Blaise d'Anjou, of all the un-American names on campus? Why a summer course? Why Tupperneck? But all of that seems massively pointless. He's Mister Private Eye. His hands are crossed as he eats his sandwich; I've never seen the like. Right hand holding the bread, and laid on the left wrist. As if even to stretch his arms out wide would invite the enemy. I can't ask him anything personal.

"Liked your girlfriend," he says as we get up to leave. "Take good care of her. And I'll see you at, say, five? In rehearsal studio E on the top floor of Pierce."

"Come on, troopers," says Faroukh. "This is the time to be good, now. You're going to be good? Right?"

The boys don't answer. Why should any boy ever answer his father?

Faroukh hoists them out of their seats and adjusts their hats. The sun has gone down, suddenly, ruefully.

He can let them run around a little more if they don't get too cold. Help them use up some of the chocolate-milk energy. The boys make that Styrofoam-crunching sound of boots in packed snow. They climb on the snowbanks as if they never saw snow back in Minneapolis.

Though he's brought warm coats for them, and boots and mittens, he carried only an Armani wool sports jacket for himself. Now he turns the collar up and stamps his loafers to keep his feet warm. He's leaking heat through his scalp, no doubt: Despite his attempts to ignore it, his hair is thinning. *I am forty*, he says to himself; *I'm trim enough, thanks to the gym and to the household need to keep the sweets at a minimum for the boys' health. My skin is good. I know who I am. The treachery of possibilities that threaten to swamp a young guy—I negotiated them. I'm on the other side. The safe side.*

Why then do I remember the perilous moments with such fond affection?

He can't answer this for himself. He only hopes his own boys are brave and lucky, to stumble into the arms of someone loving when they most need to.

He swoops them both up, surprises them from behind into whoops of laughing protest. "Time to go in," he says. "Time to get the show on the road here."

And then I am at the rehearsal-room door, and through it. And closing it. The sun is back, the rain is gone. Blaise is at the piano bench with my page of lyrics set on the rack. The air conditioner is throbbing ineffectually, making a rhythm section of its own.

"Culture Club," says Blaise. "I'm thinking, 'Do You Really Want to Hurt Me?'"

"Yes," I say.

"Something sort of quietly rhythmic, oppressive.

Paranoid. Stealing around and looking in windows. Like the new Police single. You know, 'Every Breath You Take.'"

I know it. I know the way the guitar intro evokes someone padding on rubber-heeled shoes, going about his business of surveillance. Storm or sun. Climbing up a tree and looking in a window to see what's going on.

"Do you know 'Sweet Dreams Are Made of This'?"

I can't bring myself to answer, just shake my head.

"Heard it earlier this summer in the U.K. A band called Eurythmics. Don't think it's out here yet. Kind of eerie, hastening, urgent. Anyway, that's what your lyrics make me think of." He strikes some chords against one another—a kind of hammer-sprung motion, right hand and left, not exactly the same chord but close. The effect is like that of a bird banging around in a cage.

Blaise has changed out of his wet yellow shirt from the morning. Now he's in a Tommy Hilfiger with dark and light blue stripes. The tail of the shirt drapes over the back of the piano bench. White shorts. His huaraches are kicked off in a corner of the room. His right foot arches on the pedal with a tentativeness, a tenderness that makes my stomach twist like a wet bathing suit being winched to drip on the pavement.

"Come on over. I'll play what I have."

I approach him but hang back. The room is only five feet wide and feeds into the gabled window: The electronic rehearsal piano is slotted in sideways, a letter in a mail slot. The light crowns his hair. These rooms were made for solo practicing. There's no way to be here and not be just about in his lap. Will he feel the temperature in the room rise? I stand apart.

It's all music to him; he's oblivious to me. He plays what he has. I am oblivious to it. He notices that much anyway. "What? You don't like it?"

"Play it again; I'm intrigued."

"Sit down." He points to the piano bench with his right elbow. "Here, there's room."

I perch, taking up three inches max. "It's okay, I'm not weird like that," he says. "You can move in. I'm not David Goldstone or Ian Boyle or one of *those* guys. Listen, I'm not sure about this bit—is it a bridge, is it part of the main thought?" He circles a finger around two lines.

I'm afraid I'll squeak. I shrug instead, which he can read even though we're shoulder to shoulder, noses ahead.

"You can't be cold; stop shaking," he says, and

puts his hand on my thigh. "You're jiggering around like a kindergarten boy on the playground." He plays a bass run. "Maybe it needs just a little instrumental line, about three measures, make this bit a kind of afterthought, but part of the verse, like a moral tacked on— Hey, are you all right?"

"I think I caught a cold in the pool the other day." My response to his hand has become visible under the treble register so I stand up and turn my back to him, pretending a need to stretch. I need to get away; I've already made a fool of myself once this summer. There's only so much mortification I can take.

He doesn't answer, just plays the opening phrase, adjusting it.

"Why don't you work something up, let me hear it later? I'm going to head out now." I catch myself, adding, "Maybe we could meet up later tonight. What's your dorm?"

"Busy tonight," he says. "Besides, I'm not staying on campus. We'll patch it up another time."

I'm cursing myself as I leave. I almost turn around. What is he doing once the door has swung shut? Even if I tiptoed back to look, I couldn't see: The glass panel is a milky white, translucent. I imagine his face sunk in his hands. Next second, though, before my foot has left the top step, I hear his hands working the keys. Instead of the ominous rhythmic thing he started with, he's playing the lullaby we talked about in class. *I gave my love a cherry that has no stone.* A song to play for a child falling asleep, not for an accidental slave to love standing outside your door.

The sign is simple and dignified. BLAISE D'ANJOU, and the date: black ink in a simple sans serif typeface, eight inches tall. "You're not here for d'Anjou?" asks a staff person on the granite steps leading to the bright, glassy lobby. She is wearing a lily of some sort on her woolly coat.

"Yes," says Faroukh.

She catches his irritation. "It's just, I mean, the children."

"They're with me."

But her smile is appreciative. He knows he shouldn't let himself get twitchy. He squares his shoulders and they pass through the doors into the crowded foyer.

Tod has been talking about the theater. It's clearly one of his passions. "What you'll learn, you babes in the wood, is that all plays are essentially about the passage of time. That is the secret subject of all great theater."

David Goldstone, who has become the most argumentative of the gay boys, says, "All theater is about time and all songs are about love—what is opera about, then?"

"Opera is about fabulous costumes," says Farber. "*Joke*, people. Opera is about stature. There are no operas about peasants. Even in their poverty and consumption, Mimi and Rodolfo are royalty in how they live, how they choose to live, and how they sing about it. The sisters in *Dialogue of the Carmelites* are more than nuns: They're saints. What makes them tick, what ennobles them, is the simple emotions. The less complicated, people, the more universal."

"Is everything so reducible?" says Abby Desroches. "Is this art as lowest common denominator?"

"Live a little more, and decide for yourself. For me, it's time and love," says Farber. "Speaking of time and love, where is our Monsieur d'Anjou today? It isn't like him to be absent. Another dropout? Master Rahmani, what *do* you do to your partners, I wonder?"

We all look around as if Blaise must be among us,

just in a different seat—as if none of us has noticed his absence. Hah.

So far, Faroukh sees no other small children here. He supposes it's the hour, or maybe a variation of New England protocol he hasn't identified before.

But that *is* Abby Desroches emerging from the women's room off the lobby. Her substantial hedge of hair has gone gray and tame, but it is still long, and her face is strong and mordant.

Though their eyes meet, she doesn't recognize Faroukh. How could she—they shared only six weeks of life together, and that was two decades ago. Yet Faroukh has recognized her. The obscure cost of being nonwhite: the stand-out invisibility of it. The accidental glance passes quick over, then beyond you because right-thinking people don't want to be seen to be studying you to see if you might be the only other cedar-skinned person they've ever met.

Blaise doesn't show up at the pool that afternoon, and I'm sorry I've come to swim at all. Soon I'm going to have to go back to my auntie's, and what little exercise of liberty that Laurel's arrival has conferred upon me will be done. I have a sudden thought in the locker room: Has Blaise gone off with Francesca, wherever she went? They haven't seemed to be an item, but maybe they are hiding it from us all.

I decide to keep the scheduled lab session just in case Blaise should show up. I can hear Abby on one side and Herbie on the other, and the laughing conversations they have with their lyricists. I sit at the piano bench and pick out a melody. Performance isn't my strength, but I can play a little bit. Mostly block chords in the bass, single note solo vocal line in the treble.

"Hey, Roukh." I look up at Blaise's approach. As usual his head is down, eyes slanted off center.

"You made it," I say. Shah of the obvious.

"Thought I should come." He swings the door closed. "My part of the bargain. Push over." He is the pianist, but this time I'm on the piano bench already. There's no room for me to stand between the edge of the bench and the protruding box of dead air conditioner. So I'm trapped. I can't exactly cross my legs under the piano. I hope he doesn't touch me, while I'm hoping of course that he does.

I blather like the gay boys he mocks; I can't help it. The proximity. "The class was guessing all kinds of stories about you. You'd been abducted by a Hollywood talent search crew. You've gone underground to fight crime. You and Francesca eloped."

He cuts me off with a slice of his hand; he's not in the mood. "I had family matters to deal with. They're not done yet, but I figured it'd be more normal for me to be here, and I didn't want to let you down."

"I'm, um, sorry." Does *family matters* always mean sickness? Or maybe someone had a wedding? Or had a mortgage foreclosed? Probably not that, not in his circle. Though I've lived my whole life in the U.S., I'm not confident about idioms that my parents avoid using.

"It's okay." He bangs out a mess of chords that disagree with that pronouncement, and he corrects himself. "It's not okay, I mean, but thanks."

"What is it? If you want to tell me, I mean."

"It's my sister," he says, "and I don't want to talk about it."

We sit in silence. Two, three minutes, four. About the length of a standard ballad—I know because I'm singing to myself, *I gave my love a cherry*, very slowly, to keep from doing anything rash. I imagine I can hear his vertebrae clenching; I can feel his eyelashes gumming up. *How can there be a chicken without a bone?* Anything

I do next will be the wrong thing. I stay like stone, looking at the music rack. *The story of "I love you," it has no end. A baby when it's sleeping has no crying.*

He moves first. He bangs his elbows on the keyboard and there's an intake of breath. He starts to cry a little. Quietly. Shoulders rolling, head down. I'm stuck, I can't move. But I can't ignore this. I can't even get away and go out for some toilet paper unless I stand on the bench and climb over him. The thought makes me dizzy.

The music from the rooms on either side of us gets louder, the laughing giddier. They seem to be working at dueling mazurkas. Maybe it's the protective screen of all that noise that allows Blaise suddenly to let go. Quietly but fiercely, tears are splashing on the plastic keys. "Stop, shhh, it's all right," I say, though of course it isn't all right, and what do I know anyway?

I try not to touch him—still, what can I do? The Godly Apparition is breaking apart before my eyes. It's not like me to be cold, but I can't trust myself. I'm quivering inside like a struck bell.

Then I don't have to make the decision. He is turning to me and driving his face into my neck. My arms have no choice but to surround him—if they don't, I'll fall off the bench and bang my head on the air conditioner. "Hey, whoa," I say in a whisper. "It's okay, Blaise. Whatever's wrong, it's okay."

He leans into me and I can't help it, my hands grip the fabric of his shirt to keep from falling backward. He is shuddering now and his arms are around me, one hand at my hip, the other circling the back of my neck, as if cradling me, protecting me. He's the one who's upset; I should be protecting him. "Stop," I whisper, and we are kissing each other on the neck at precisely the same instant. We pull apart. His characteristic *froideur* is blasted apart with grief of some obscure variety—and me? Me? I'm trying not to take advantage of the situation.

It's almost like nausea, the way lust rises so saltily, and I keep trying to swallow it down. "What?" I say. That's the last word I say. Our eyes lock before our mouths do; and now he is falling backward off the bench onto the floor, and pulling me after him. There are two or three moments of wrestling—from a distance you would think we were antagonists—then he pulls away. In revulsion, I think; his fit is over and sobriety has set in, and repugnance will follow. If there's any justice he'll break my middle finger.

But he's only bounded up to lock the door. When he turns to fall upon me his buttoned sleeve catches on the doorknob. The sleeve rips right out from the shoulder. It doesn't stop him. Nothing stops him. Nothing stops me. His thighs are clenching my hips, his blond forelocks sweeping my lashes, his hands working under my T-shirt, walking up my chest as if he wishes I were a woman, and he bucks against me, instrumentally. The twin mazurkas couching us from either side have become frenzied cacophony.

It is my first real kiss. We have exactly nine days left.

The hall is thronged and the buzz is soft and dignified, like a cocktail party for retirees. In the front of the room stands a baby grand with a vase of a dozen roses on its closed top. Tupperneck never had that kind of instrument, not for the students to play around with anyway. A light is trained on the roses. Everything is plain, a kind of stage set. A music stand and a microphone. A table with a decanter and a glass of water in which a lime swims among the ice.

The back row is mostly filled. "Would you mind terribly moving up a row?" Faroukh whispers to an elderly couple befogged in colognes of competing strengths. "I feel I should be back here, close to the exit in case of a noisy moment."

The woman sniffs. "Come, Gerty," says her husband. "We'll hear no better one row up, don't worry."

They shift themselves. Faroukh settles in and wrestles the boys out of their heavy parkas.

"I'm thirsty," says Matthias. Faroukh produces the sippy cup.

"Tirsty," says Jamesy.

"Share," says Faroukh. Uncharacteristically obedient, Matthias nods and hands the cup over. The sobriety in the room is calming to them, palpable. It's the hush of expectation. Though they don't know what to expect. Neither, for so much of his life, has Faroukh.

It takes me several days of asking questions—slowly, letting the answers steep before pushing on—to learn what has happened to Blaise. Little by little it comes clear—his distance, his isolation. He is an American kid living overseas these past six years, in Toulouse— the son of a French father and an American mother. His older sister, Monette, and her husband and their daughter, Cecile, disappeared several months ago in a small private plane that went down in the Mediterranean. Off the coast of Sardinia. It was clear they were dead; what else could have happened? Blaise's parents have come to Monette's lake house north of Tupperneck to reclaim family items before the home is gussied up and put on the market. Blaise has come along to be company—because in their loss they couldn't stand to leave him in France—but he can't tolerate their endless weeping. He's struck a compromise: He will take a summer course locally, get out of the cottage several times a week.

This week, finally, bits of identifiable wreckage have begun to wash up on shore. Airplane fuselage, some luggage. This has rendered baseless any remaining hopes that no news might yet be good news.

"So now—you'll go home?" I ask.

"There's more to do," Blaise replies, "but my parents are stepping up the schedule. Up till now it's been like, treasure every spoon, every photo, every recipe. Now everything's going in boxes or garbage bags: save or surrender. They can't bear the task anymore, all at once. They'll be done by the time the semester finishes."

We are facing each other, sitting on the floor in the locked rehearsal room. I am in briefs, my legs locked

HOW BEAUTIFUL THE ORDINARY

310

about his waist; he is cool and clothed. I touch his knees, running my hands in his loose shorts, meaning comfort, but he misreads me as merely horny, and flinches. I freeze. I meant to say, *You have me; I'm not your dead family but I'm here, alive, yours.* I take his reaction to mean, *I can't afford to confuse grief and love, or I'll explode.*

What he also means—and I understand this little by little—little trial, big error—is that we will keep our romantic alliance a secret. In class we choose to ignore each other. We keep to our original seats, neither arriving together nor leaving together.

I'm not quite sure why. It isn't that anyone would disapprove, not in this crowd. I suppose it's that we haven't got time to include anyone else. Nine days. Eight days. Seven.

Tod Farber especially can't learn what's going on. He would mind—he would be jealous, says Blaise. He's never been inappropriate, nothing like that. Just louche. Just campy. It's all insinuation.

"Why does he bother? He doesn't know you're in mourning. You only registered as . . . as so . . . aloof," I whisper.

"How would you know what I registered as? You

never glanced at me. While I sat behind you and watched at how your dark hair turns almost red when the sun strokes it—you were the icy one, never turning to give me the time of day. Everyone else did. Farber, and Francesca, and the Gay Boys Student League."

I don't want to hear about Francesca Comstock. She seemed rare enough to appeal to Blaise and it was just my luck, this once, that she stalked away, leaving me an opening.

Six days. Every evening Blaise takes the shuttle bus that the town puts on for summer folk and he returns to Monette's lake house. Every night I walk back to Auntie Nurjahan's—I can't bear being around Herbie Manzella right now. But this isn't good enough.

Once we go to the pool, arriving separately, but that's a mistake we realize almost at once. Our mutual attraction would be a matter of public record to anyone paying the barest of attention, and everyone pays attention to Blaise. He leaves first, his towel wrapped securely around his waist. I stay in the pool. Doing laps, cooling off. It isn't good enough.

On the fifth day we make a plan that might work. Nobody mops up Pierce Hall during the summer. No Korean lady with a vacuum and spray polish. We've scoped it out: The night security detail comes through sometime between nine and ten. So we hang out in Pierce, in Rehearsal Room E in the attics on the third floor. At 9 P.M. we turn out the light. We lie low—literally. The guard can see as he passes the door that the lights inside are off. If he tries the door—which one night he does, causing us to clench each other the harder as we lie on the floor, entwined in the dark—he finds it locked.

We lie all night in each other's arms, in a heap of blankets Blaise has borrowed from a cupboard in the lake house. If we need to use the bathroom or even shower, we do it in the dark. Not a single light to signal a midnight presence to any campus cop driving around bored. Not a candle, a flashlight, a match.

And we get nervy. This place was a home, after all, once upon a time. And a well-appointed home. It still has a kitchen and a fridge, a bathroom with a huge, old clawfooted tub. At four in the morning we move the extra music stands out of the tub and rinse out the dust, and find a plug, and run the water. We turn to each other in the only light there is; we feel for each other with hands that have learned to be bold, to possess without apology.

We roam the place in the dark, holding hands, finding new corners in which to kiss. It is our own home, our imagined otherlife in the dark.

And we make out; it's exciting. Once on Farber's desk in Pierce 203.

Blaise asks about Laurel Finn. I keep my words to a minimum. If Blaise can be so circumspect about his emotional entanglements, why can't I? "It's over, at least for now," I say. "I'm not thinking of Laurel right now. What about you? Why are you so hoity about the chorus boy wannabes when you know perfectly well what they're up to, and you're up to it too?"

"I'm not being holier-than-thou," says Blaise. "I'm just tired of everyone trying to jump my bones all the time. You're the only guy in this group who has an evident girlfriend. I think that's why I could risk touching you when I was losing it that afternoon. I knew you wouldn't take advantage."

I didn't answer that. "Still, is it an act? An anti-gay thing so as to throw off suspicion?"

"I don't know what it is." However brilliant Blaise is at international life, however highly Tod Farber regards Blaise's compositional strengths, Blaise seems oddly clueless about himself. Almost deferential to his own confusions. "I just don't expect much except people wanting something out of me."

"But what do you want? Stop; *besides* that. Really."

"Mmmm. This." And as often as not it isn't the sex, or put another way, it's what comes after and before the sex: It's the animal purr that the human body imitates, the animal comfort. It's boys in the treehouse being together against the adults. It's the game of being nonchalant in front of Herbie and Abby and David and the others. I don't know how to name it any better than Blaise does, I guess. I just finally know how to recognize it when it stares me in the face.

A girl in a black skirt and a white shirt comes through, passing out programs. There is a picture of Blaise on the front, a studio shot for publicity purposes.

Faroukh is knocked sideways, the formality of it. He has only seen Blaise once after saying good-bye at Tupperneck. It was eight years later, when they were both about twenty-six. Blaise had begun to rise, perhaps not yet meteorically but definitely. Faroukh was in his third and final year as a middle-school English teacher.

A letter had come from a literary agent, and another letter from an entertainment lawyer. Mr. d'Anjou had written a song based on lyrics of Mr. Rahmani's, and would like permission to buy them outright or, barring that, to settle on a royalty split of 75–25 in favor of the composer, given the Grammy nomination and the forthcoming album, as yet untitled, due in the stores next Christmas.

Faroukh had made the big mistake of mentioning it to his father, who had proposed accompanying his son to Manhattan to sign the agreements. "You are sweet boy," said his baba, "yet you know nothing about money." And it was true that Baba and Maman had surprisingly managed to amass enough money or credit in the intervening years to buy four rental units, and all on Baba's salary as a janitor.

"But there's no need," Faroukh had said. "Once we decide on terms, we can execute the documents by mail."

"Is better in person," said Baba, and Faroukh realized his father was grasping at a legitimate reason to visit the big city. Baba would not indulge himself in pleasures, and so Faroukh couldn't deny him this one. He made the hotel booking only after confirming that an executor for Mr. d'Anjou would sign the contract since the artist would be out of the country at the time.

Mr. Rahmani dyed his moustache a regrettably uniform black and bought a suit jacket at the Salvation Army. Faroukh and his father traveled together by Amtrak to the big city. They found an Iranian restaurant on West End Avenue where the waiters spoke Farsi, and Faroukh's baba wept at the sound of it. And at the ripe pomegranates on the table. And at the pungent beads of *zereshk* added to the rice, smelling like Dizbad, smelling like Mashad, smelling like home.

The next day they arrived at the lawyer's office. Forty-five minutes after the scheduled appointment time, they were shown into a large conference room with a photocopy machine in the corner and a tray of fancy pastries simultaneously softening and crusting over on the windowsill. With a flourish Yusuf Rahmani brought out the rosewater *loukoumia* that his wife had made to sweeten the deal. No one took a piece.

This would not take long, said the lawyers, and indeed they were halfway through the short stack of documents when an executive assistant opened the door and announced, "Blaise d'Anjou is passing through and wants to swing in?" and the bigwigs nodded. At once Blaise was in the doorway, before Faroukh could even rise. Blaise took in Rahmani *père et fils* with one sweep of his eyes. He was accompanied by a cunning young man in a good cut of designer jeans. Dancer type.

Faroukh didn't remember the words, exactly how it happened; Blaise clearly hadn't expected this encounter. He reddened and stammered an apology for intruding and backed up. "We'll have our reunion another time, soon," he claimed, "later," and disappeared. Faroukh couldn't read it; he'd never been good at that kind of thing and still wasn't. It was like an apparition, little more than that.

So he was more than surprised when, a half hour later, on his way back from the men's room at the end of the hall, Blaise appeared from behind a column and pushed him into a walk-in cloak room. Pushed him, back and back into the depths of the room, out of sight, against a row of hangers on which hung men's and women's good winter coats strongly powdered with scent of cologne and mothballs. Blaise threw his arms around Faroukh's waist in the dark, as if it was the same dark as in Pierce eight years earlier. He gripped Faroukh's behind and hoisted him up against the coats with such force that stitches ripped in the seat of Faroukh's new trousers. Faroukh had to flail to grab a hanger, a coathook, to keep from falling backward. "You!" panted Blaise, "You! *You!*"

"Are you mad?" Farouk had hissed back, kissing his lost friend, kicking for his lost footing, grabbing for a hold of his lost lover. Blaise was already hot and seconds shy of a mess.

That evening they'd managed two hours more in a hotel room on lower Madison Avenue, escaped from their mutual obligations through various pretexts of one sort or other. The other guy, Faroukh learned, was the brother of Blaise's girlfriend. Faroukh didn't ask any more. There were too many ways to be hurt.

"Call me. Or I'll call you," said Blaise. "Later. Later." But stupefied with a relief that was already vanishing, with regret already setting in, Faroukh let Blaise's phone number drift onto the subway track of the Number 1 as he hurried back to his father.

"Is nice," said his baba on the train home next morning. Faroukh wanted the conversation to be about Blaise. He held his breath. "Is very nice," said Baba, looking away, looking out the window. "But is no Teheran."

The Blaise in the photo tonight is yet again older but still recognizably potent. A look of interior complexity that might be conceit. That perfect nose. A chin that has grown a cleft, how odd. Could Hollywood people have clefts dug surgically?

"Who dat?" asked Matthias, looking over Faroukh's forearm at the paper. The people sitting nearby look away, clearly hoping Matthias isn't going to pepper the evening with adorable childish interpolations.

We are nearing the close of our magic week in our dark, private house. Blaise is saying, "So when we finish, it's back to France."

"To college?"

"A kind of gap year. I think I want to go to college in the States, but what with the tragedy I didn't get everything in on schedule. Maybe I'll railpass around the continent and get some pickup gigs. Or hang out in Toulouse and do some busking for the tourists this autumn."

I want him to say, *Come with me. Come to France. Come away.* I wait for him to say it.

"And you're reading English at Colchester." He makes it sound as if I'm going into the mopping of floors at Sisters of Charity. I don't want to do Colchester anymore, after all this. I want to go to Europe with Blaise. I want this to be the start of my life.

Imagine Baba when I tell him. If I tell him. If I get the chance to tell him.

Imagine if Blaise comes back to Buffalo with me. Blaise sitting on the floor, Iranian style, in our walk-through flat with no furniture in the front rooms but beautiful Persian carpets and a photograph of the Imam; nothing in the bedroom but mattresses and books in Farsi; nothing in the kitchen—Maman still rinses rice in a big aluminum bowl while squatting on the floor—nothing but the smell of holy Iran. Nothing but the Silk Road, and where it has brought us.

And a big American television, on which we will see Blaise perform one day—but we don't know that yet.

I imagine holding his hand on the carpet. I imagine him making them blush with pride, that he could choose a boy like me. I imagine rose petals on the floor; Maman is not above that when she has a mind to be joyful. And when her headaches abate.

While I can hope for it, I already know it is impossible. For now, we have the impossible present, and I try to focus. We're in the deep window seat on the stair landing, sitting naked with our legs entwined. The outside campus security lamplight comes in through the diamond-paned glass; the mullions make slanted parallelograms across Blaise's ivory chest into the mauve shadows of his groin. He puts his arms up behind his head and rests like that. I could stretch out a toe and tickle him in the armpit; we could romp and roll right here on the corduroy cushions. But the mood isn't right. He feels my unasked question and doesn't answer it.

Instead he says, "You'll go back to your Laurel in September, I guess."

My Laurel. Hmmm. "I guess not."

"Sure you will. I could tell by how she looked at you—"

"How she looked . . ." I try not to sound vicious, just sort of curious about myself. "Laurel and I have some bad history behind us and I don't want to revisit it. Besides—that was—before—all this. You know?"

"This is just this," he says. "You're aware of that, Faroukh. I'm sure you know that."

"I don't know much," I say, very slowly, very tentatively. "I know what I feel. I don't even know what I can imagine. But I couldn't imagine sleeping with you, and it happened anyway. So maybe there's more to happen that I can't picture yet." *Maman. Baba. This is Blaise. My new life.*

"There is more ahead for us, of course. We'll have

this accidental romance. It'll be packed away like, um. Like Monette's photographs, like Cecile's crayon drawings. We'll have this passage to take out and listen to. To admire. You're not thinking anything beyond the summer. Faroukh?"

My face is as steel as I can make it. Loving, pleading steel.

"*Roukh*. Be real. There's all the rest of life out there. This is—this is the intro. The prelude. Maybe it announces the theme even—but we'll pick up the theme in a different key next time around."

I don't even have to say it. Next time around? What, the afterlife?

But I must say something. "You kiss me, you console me, all that, all that"—my hands flailing in the dark mean *the sex the sex the sex*—"and it's a diversion? What's the main event then, after this? Are you becoming a bishop or a senator or something where it matters?"

"Don't be pissy. You're sounding like the Gay Club. You know perfectly well—"

"I am sounding like someone stranded in about an acre of shit." In my panic I am sounding, frankly, like Laurel. The words and also the wobble in the voice;

phlegmy. My eyes spill.

"I want a family. Of course. I want to have kids. I want someone to give Monette's spoons to someday. After all that has happened to my parents? Losing Monette and their granddaughter? Don't you think I have any heart? Are you out of your mind?"

The very words I said to Laurel Finn. The very words.

How can you argue against the desire for children? I don't have it, but I recognize it when I see it. Laurel Finn has it: hence her delusion about pregnancy. "You could join the Big Brothers of America. We could get a dog. . . ."

"We're going to be a couple with a dog? Faroukh, hello, stop right there—where'd you get this picture? This isn't Gay Lifestyle 101 we're taking at Tupperneck Community Day Care—it's music and lyrics—it's an interlude—it's a bridge—"

"It's a fucking sham, is that what you're saying?" I am on my knees, profiled against the window, when the key turns in the lock of Pierce and the door swings open.

Freeze or flee. If we dart upstairs to our clothes, someone will follow us, find us out. I can't afford to be tossed out of Tupperneck and jeopardize my financial aid to Colchester. Blaise—by his own admission—doesn't want to be known as a homo on the side. Our eyes lock, unblinking. Not a muscle flexes in either of us; we have communicated to each other the same strategy. *Marble statue.* Maybe whoever it is won't glance up the staircase. Will pick up the mail from the faculty slot or root around for some files in the secretary's carrel underneath where the stairs turn, and then go out.

Steps on the creaking floorboards from the former parlor—now a seminar room—to the scratched baby grand piano berthed in the large bay window beyond. The thing, we know, is padlocked with a grotesque industrial hinge stapled right into the wood. Someone is unlocking it and sitting down—in the dark—and starting to play.

It's Tod Farber. You learn someone's playing style in ten minutes. He was an accomplished performer once, but he's slurring his notes, not so much jazzily as drunkenly. He takes at a glacial clip a few of his favorite standards from the forties. "Just One of Those Things." It sounds like funeral music.

I look at Blaise to see if he wants to move. Shall we

risk skittering up to our aerie, having Tod Farber hear our naked feet on the stairs? Blaise looks frozen, not so much terrified as bewildered. Perhaps he's shocked that Farber has stumbled in to provide mood music for our breakup. "Just One of the Those Things," a song of good-bye without regrets. Farber adds a bluesy cadence and the laziest sort of New Orleans stride—he's improvising between each line.

Blaise d'Anjou leans his head back against the wallpaper imprisoned by the shadowy fretwork. It is his turn to cry, but the music is doing the work for him. He can't do it for himself. He doesn't look at me; he doesn't tremble as I do when I cry. He's Blaise. He's a bronze statue in the fake moonlight of the amber-colored sulfur lights on the campus. I reach my hand across the distance, touch his shoulder, let my hand trail down his slightly twisted trunk, and feed my finger very lightly into the top of the cleft between the cheeks of his ass. Nothing saucier than that. My little fingerhold has always seemed the most vulnerable inch on his brave young body, his chevalier physique. And I have had experience with vulnerability.

After a while Farber gets up and stumbles out. Blaise and I don't speak to each other. We gather our clothes and leave by a back door. No one sees us. No one will ever see us.

"Ladies and gentlemen. On behalf of the board of governors, may I welcome you to the New England Fiduciary Hall of the Tupperneck Arts Division of the State University. What a distinct privilege it is to greet you all here as we gather to honor the work of one of the preeminent composers of our time. Some may ask, why now, and we say, why not? We remember fifteen years of distinctive contribution to the world of music. It is a short period, so far, but what is time to us? Look what, in his thirty-five years, Mozart managed to give us. Sam Cooke at thirty-three, Gershwin at thirty-eight. Stephen Foster at thirty-eight. Chopin at thirty-nine.

"But I refer toward the morbid as a way to make a point. We are not here to mourn but to celebrate. Music is eternal, and in the fifteen years of the professional life of Blaise d'Anjou we have seen him help the revival of the art song. We've enjoyed his contributions to serious film scoring. We've seen several popular entries to the top forty, fighting their way against the banality of hip-hop and what I like to think of as techno-coma. I see I offend. How sweet."

There is a polite laugh. Most of the crowd is his own age or older. People with money. People to hit up for funds when the time is right. At the funeral last month, Auntie Nurjahan had mentioned hearing word of this fund-raiser, remembering that my one small contribution to American arts had involved Blaise d'Anjou. She's right about the crowd it would draw. Silvery curls and shining pates and old women with nostrils that splay wide, three inches above their sunken lips. A lot of jewelry.

Farber hasn't changed all that much. "I see faces in the crowd here I believe I recognize, but I shall not embarrass you by singling you out for honor or opprobrium." More polite laughter, a little impatient by now. Farber seems to hear this; he was always smart. "Let us proceed then, ladies and gentlemen, will you join me . . . ?"

I have to make an appointment to see Professor Tod Farber. "I need to take an incomplete, I guess."

"You've handed in your assignments on time," says Tod Farber. "The class is over in two days. You can't possibly be behind on your work. And as I remember— am I right, dear boy?—you had something of a crisis, needing this course under your belt?"

We're sitting in Farber's office on the ground floor of Pierce. The secretary is ordering manila folders for the start of the fall semester. New personnel are around, reclaiming the building. Out the open door I can just see the cushioned window seat on the stair landing. Someone has left on it a snarl of vacuum cleaner attachments. The air smells of Windex and panic.

"There's the final composition. I'm supposed to do it with Blaise d'Anjou." I can't say d'Anjou in a French way yet. Tod Farber winces.

"Yes. Monsieur *d'Anjou*, our season's maestro of melodic invention."

"We can't work together. It's just not working."

Professor Farber raises one eyebrow almost drolly. "It seemed to my distant and tired eye you were getting along like a house on fire. Quite the little *tendresse*, of a purely aesthetic collaborative nature I mean. You were suited, perhaps, is the better word. I'd been looking forward to being the midwife to a new Lennon and McCartney. Rodgers and Hart. D'Anjou and Rahmani. No? Pity. *Quel dommage.* Surely you can patch it up for this final project?"

I don't want to spill my heart to Farber, of all people.

I'd rather lose the financial aid. One crisis a summer ought to be enough. "I've done my work," I say. "He's not talking to me now."

"Tsk-tsk. The heartbeats of the young. It's all love songs, I am always telling you boys and girls, but no one ever listens."

"He's had a family emergency," I say. This isn't it, but well, it is. It's true enough. It's part of what has happened between us, as far as I can understand it now.

"Is your part done?"

"I have a lyric," I tell him. "But the way Blaise and I were working—it gets refined and revised at the keyboard. And he's not available."

"I'm not prying. I'm not prying one little bit, Faroukh."

I'm a lyricist now: I can lie easy as anything. "He won't say anything to you about his sister, I think. He's very private. But she died in the spring, in a plane crash."

"Ah. Mortality. And of course that's at the heart of all love songs—but I see I bore you. That's my prerogative of course—I have the tenure to prove it—but let us be positive. If you will surrender your lyric to me and if I think it merits the credit, I will pass on the text to

Monsieur d'Anjou when I see him. Perhaps when his spirits lift, he can do something with it. I don't see that you should be faulted for his emotional frailties."

I hand over the piece. Professor Farber glances at it. "Short."

"Pithy," I reply. "'Moon River' is short. 'Over the Rainbow' is short. You can say a lot in a few words."

"If you've grown up enough to know what's worth saying. Have you grown up that much this summer, Master Rahmani?"

"'Yesterday' is short. Very short."

"I see you have."

He takes a pen and adds my name to the top; I haven't remembered that little bit. There's a lot to learn about being lost in the world, including putting a tag on yourself in case anyone ever wants to find you.

Not that I am expecting Blaise d'Anjou will ever want that.

Tod seems to be prolonging this. "The rhythm is very common and I can't say the rhyme scheme is all that adventurous."

"I modeled it on Emily Dickinson's poetry. She used the scansions of hymn tunes for her model. I figured I could turn it back to a hymn. Of sorts."

"What did I say to you about the last word needing to be an open vowel, so that the next reigning diva can hold out the final note for sixteen bars?"

"I made an aesthetic decision."

"A compromise or a decision? Hmmm." He reads it through again; I watch his eyes moving down the page. In a softer voice. "It has a title?"

"Oh, sorry. It's the first line—I mean the first half of the first line."

"'For What It's Worth.'"

"Yeah."

He smiles wryly. "Well, for what's it worth, Faroukh, I'm guessing you had a memorable summer here at Tupperneck. I hope you come back someday."

"Professor Farber," I say, standing up and putting out my hand for a shake, "I doubt I ever will."

Only as I'm out again on the lawns—now dried to scratchy sedge after our burnt-out summer—do I wonder if Tod Farber thinks that he was the subject of the lyric. Well, no harm if he does.

The boys respond to the lowering lights by climbing in Faroukh's lap and standing on his thighs so he can't see at first.

Tod Farber twitches a finger and a stocky male undergraduate in white shirt and black trousers comes out and opens the piano lid. The student takes his place seated on a chair by the side of the piano bench. Page turner. He *doesn't get to sit on the same bench as Blaise d'Anjou,* thinks Faroukh. Then the guest of honor comes out from behind a curtain.

Since that accidental reunion in the New York law office, Faroukh has only seen Blaise in the magazines and on *Entertainment Tonight*. He knows how the cheeks have thickened a little, how the shiny gold hair is already threaded with silver. But thick as ever. Faroukh runs a hand over his own scalp, aerating what's left; he can't stop himself. But grins as he does it. Grimly.

Men at forty don't wear the kinds of clothes that boys at eighteen wear in the summer. Faroukh can't tell much about how Blaise has filled out. But a tux does no one any harm, especially someone a little swollen with success.

Blaise doesn't speak. He sits and plays. Faroukh finds his eyes dimly wet—not the blatant springs of new, young pain, just an emotive dampness appropriate to a man entering his middle years.

The short program details the compositions. Most of them Faroukh has heard, either on the soundtracks of rented DVDs from Netflix or, once in a while, on the classical program on NPR. And of course the several genre-busting popular songs, beginning to be covered by the great chanteuses of the day. None of *them* are here raising money for the music department of the State University, Faroukh notices. But then, why would they? They didn't live a whole life for five nights in a rehearsal studio on the top floor of Pierce.

There will be no intermission, he notices. He hasn't been able to hope he might hear the whole thing, but it won't be long—forty-five minutes, tops. The university knows that allowing donors to schmooze with the talent will prove additionally lucrative in the long run.

The *Danse Intime.* An elegant melody, a fugue written forward and then played backward.

The *Adagio for 9/11.* How could a musician just forty know that such a melody lived inside the piano? Had it always lived there until Blaise d'Anjou found it? And had Blaise found it because of what he knew about loss—of his sister, his niece—of anyone he had ever loved deeply?

Faroukh Rahmani is weeping more openly, but he's not alone.

And that is that. The rounds of applause. Faroukh

stands with his boys in his arms, and since he can't clap, he finds himself hooting. He doesn't know if Blaise will hear his voice in the crowd, or recognize it. He won't stay for the wine and cheese. He got what he came for.

Blaise returns. The crowd sits down for an encore the program doesn't advertise. The young man who has been turning the piano music steps forward. He goes to the music stand opposite the piano.

Blaise says, "Though I'm not much for public speaking, I have to say this much. The encore was written here—on the Tupperneck campus, back when it was still an independent college. Guess the fund-raising back then didn't work as efficiently as it will tonight."

This time the polite titters are a little nervous.

Blaise sits down and goes right into the famous opening. Three quarters of the crowd are probably seeing Angela Bassett in that sequence used for the titles. Faroukh only sees Blaise diamonded by the streetlight, age eighteen forever.

The young man at the music stand sings in a blameless but ineffectual baritone.

> *"For what it's worth, I love you.*
> *I hope someday you know.*

These words so roundly overdue
I whispered long ago.

"For what it's worth, I mention
A secret never shared.
I never asked for your attention.
I never dared.

"Of all the things that might be true
Of all I've said upon the earth,
I love you most, and still I do,
For what it's worth."

The lyrics are an eighteen-year-old's, unnaturally old-fashioned. They don't even make much sense. Still, the older Faroukh gets, the more his own juvenile words mean to him. Was it Noel Coward who said, "Astonishing, the potency of cheap music"? Something like that.

Professor Tod Farber is leading the applause. Matthias says, "I peed in my snow pants." Faroukh ducks out with his boys.

I see Blaise once more before I leave. He is crossing the lawn to a parking lot, moving fast as if he doesn't intend to be recognized or intercepted. Abby Desroches is all but jogging next to him, trying to say something enticing. I know that look.

I can't help myself; I start to wave, as if my small gesture will somehow register just because it's me. Hey, look! Blaise d'Anjou! It's Faroukh Rahmani, remember? From last week? Your incidental boyfriend? Your secret passion for nine days straight? Though maybe *straight* isn't the best word.

He has seen me. He turns and jogs in place, pointing to his wristwatch. "Got your address from the registrar. I'm *way* ahead of you. I'll write after I get back to France. Promise. Roukh, I promise. But I have to fly. Morgan Goodwill's coming with a truck to the house at noon today and my folks can't deal; it's all coming down around my head. . . . Later. *Later!*"

And again he is running forward, running away. He is running toward his children, his wife, the future that will formally compensate for the loss that he and his parents suffered this summer. I was the accidental lover. We all take advantage of each other.

Professor Tod Farber confers upon me a B plus. I persuade Colchester to reinstate my financial aid. I buy a new duffel bag. I move through my days like a person who has had a stroke. Baba doesn't ask what's wrong. Once he says, "I hear Laurel Finn is seeing counselor from school. She will study to be nurse. Good work for single woman who wants so much for baby she doesn't have. Yet." I think that is as much an apology as he can muster. I'm glad for it but I can't answer. I go sit on the roof over the garage and get some sun. There is nothing left for me but college and grown-up life. I might as well roll off the roof and snap my spine and die in the ferns that have already crisped up in the oven of the summer.

I pretend I'm not waiting for the phone to ring. When it does ring and it's for me, it's never Blaise. It's always Auntie Nurjahan in tears, braying about how much she misses me.

I can't listen to the radio for almost a year. Crafty old Farber ended up being right: Every song is a love song.

Faroukh is done; he's had enough. But Matthias has lost the sippy somewhere, and he threatens to raise the roof with his grief. There's nothing for it but that Faroukh has to skulk back into the room with two boys, one under each arm, to hunt for it. The crew is clearing away the folding chairs. Side doors Faroukh hadn't noticed are being opened in stiff, ugly accordion pleats, like huge ribs of cardboard, revealing a sumptuous reception. Candlelight and cheese platters and waiters circulating with hot hors d'oeuvres. Matthias decides, sensibly, something more or less like *fuck the sippy*, and he breaks free to dart toward the goodies.

"I thought I saw a familiar form," says Tod Farber.

Odd, they seem to be the same height now. "You're still here."

"Here isn't here anymore, it's the university. A much better pension package, for one thing. And yes, I'm the department chair this year. You haven't stayed in music, have you—" And Faroukh sees that Professor Farber doesn't remember that the lyrics of the famous sentimental pop song are written by Faroukh Rahmani, and date from that summer course.

"No. I'm, um, self-employed in the Twin Cities. I manage real estate from home."

"Shocking. Have you seen our guest of honor yet?"

"No. I saw him from a distance; that's enough."

Tod Farber takes a sip of wine. "You were the same summer, weren't you? Do I have that right? I taught that course so many times. He hasn't seen you, or he'd be over here in a flash."

"He doesn't recognize me. I'm surprised you do."

"Of course *I'd* recognize you anywhere. That lithe and lovely form."

Faroukh isn't eighteen anymore. "You sound downright lecherous, Professor Farber."

"I never laid a hand on a student," says Tod Farber placidly. "I knew my place. But I could look, couldn't I? And if boys will prance naked around the music building in the middle of the night, it's not because I handed out any assignment requiring them to do it."

Faroukh grabs Jamesy by the hand to keep him from tripping up a waitress carrying spring rolls. "I don't know what you're talking about."

"Well, I wasn't the one climbing up into the maple tree in the middle of the night," he replies. "Was I? Looking in the windows?"

"I don't know," Faroukh says. "Were you?"

As I'm climbing down, having seen nothing in the dark window, I can also see no one in the dark shadows. Professor Farber always wears black, of course. Black rayon, an odd choice for such a blisteringly hot summer.

Faroukh is in the lobby busy shucking the boys into their coats. The noise in the reception room increases in volume as people lurch for their third glasses of champagne. But for Faroukh the adventure is over. The boys are beginning to lose it. They will be asleep in the car in minutes. Back to the Marriott Courtyard. Tomorrow, back down the highway several hours to the Avis depot at Logan. Back halfway across the country to the sweet surcease of the hip and happening Twin Cities. Something has finished that needed to be finished, that wasn't finished the time Faroukh and Blaise met in New York.

Faroukh feels as tired as his boys. Jamesy is almost asleep on his shoulder. If someone could only pick *him* up and carry him . . .

Matthias can't get his arm in his parka because it has gotten twisted up with the strings from the mittens. If Faroukh lays Jamesy down he'll pop back awake and wail. It's a monkey puzzle of an effort, needing another pair of hands.

"May I help?"

Faroukh is on his knees and looks up. Blaise has come out of the men's room situated off the lobby. He's not looking at Faroukh. His eyes are on

Matthias twisted in his winter wear.

"I never say no to help."

Blaise is fiddling with the mitten, turning it right, winking at skeptical Matthias. Then the certain music of Faroukh's voice hits the musician's brain. Blaise swivels his head. His eyes widen. This close, Faroukh can scrutinize the bags under Blaise's eyes; also the very faint hint of eyeliner.

A week before Baba died of his heart attack—a month ago now, the longest month of Farouk's life—they have invited Faroukh's parents to see the new Ang Lee film, *Brokeback Mountain*. It's still packing the small art house they frequent, and Faroukh hopes the presence of a general audience will soothe his parents somewhat. Faroukh and Jake have already seen it, so Faroukh knows what his parents are in for. Faroukh wants to complete something he never completed. His father has given him so much—the money to buy his first rental, the distance that has allowed him to grow into himself—Faroukh wants to pay him back with a kind of honesty, at last, that his parents might understand.

They have never cared for films, but in their old age, removed from Tonawanda and living in Minneapolis on the generosity of Faroukh and Jake, they accept the invitation without complaint. Faroukh and Jake cry harder the second time. Afterward they take Baba and Maman out for an Indian meal. When the basmati rice has come steaming to the table and the chicken korma is being passed around, Jake says, "What did you make of it, Mr. and Mrs. R?"

Both Yusuf and Amina Rahmani have raw eyes. They are not abashed by emotion at this stage of their lives. "Is good movie-film," says Baba, looking back and forth between his son and his son's husband. He tears up.

Maman puts her hand upon her husband's on the tabletop. She says to them all, "Those boys in movie-film such good friends. Why not their wives be good friends too?"

Jake grins. "Why not? I never know the answer to questions like that."

But now Baba is crying harder. It has taken a while for the film to get to him. "What is it, Baba?" asks Faroukh. Maybe this wasn't such a good idea. "We're all right, Baba. We're all here. Your best little boys are home safe with the sitter. What's the matter?"

Yusuf Rahmani blows his nose and sips some water.

He says. "You do not understand. The sheep on sides of hills—the sky singing with wind. I am homesick. This is my boyhood. This movie-film is made in Iran."

"Not possible," Blaise says to solemn Matthias. "Not possible that this voice is your, um, your—"

"Your dad's," Faroukh supplies. He stands up. "Hey there, Blaise. I was trying to sneak out."

"If I'd have known you were here," says Blaise, "I'd have given you the credit for the lyric."

"No matter. The lyric is hogwash without the melody."

"It means so much to me."

"It means a lot to me. That annual royalty check on a little tiny chromosomal twitch of popular culture . . ." Not enough to live on, not enough to boast about, but enough to appreciate from time to time if Faroukh starts feeling low.

The whole building is abuzz with celebratory glee, and somehow they are alone in the lobby. Alone but for the boys.

"How old are you, you fine fellow?" Blaise asks Matthias. The bleary kid raises a hand to display a number of raised fingers, but the hand is already mittened against the cold. "Oh," says Blaise. "That many already?" Matthias nods.

"How long are you here?" Blaise asks Faroukh.

"I was leaving ten minutes ago." Faroukh is not working at being cool. The kids' exhaustion dictates what happens next. There is no other option. They are his life.

"But Roukh—" And Faroukh has forgotten that that was Blaise's nickname for him, that he'd been given a nickname. It had been buried. *Roukh*. "You can't—you can't. This won't last long. I've done my bit. I'm not committed beyond another half hour, tops. We can slip out—"

"*Mon coeur*," says a voice, someone emerging from the women's room. A tapering flame of a woman with hair so fine it looks almost translucent, coiled like the thinnest sort of fiber-optic filament on her head. Baked into a solid form. She is weird and stunning. Faroukh didn't notice her in the hall. Maybe she was sipping green tea backstage somewhere.

"Darling," says Blaise. "Come here. An old, dear friend in the business. Faroukh Rahmani."

Faroukh puts forth a hand. She raises hers in a sanitary salute, eschewing contact.

"My wife," says Blaise. "Katrín Minervudóttir."

Well, thinks Faroukh. *Her name isn't Mary Lou Polka-Dot from Tulsa, Oklahoma. Big surprise.*

"*Enchanté,*" says Blaise's wife, as if she does mean it, but intends to mean little more than that. "Will you be long?" she says to her husband.

"I'm leaving right now," interjects Faroukh.

She smiles beautifully, but she is talking to her husband.

"Not at all. Minutes only, darling," says Blaise.

"As you wish. *Au revoir, Monsieur—*" Katrín can't attempt a name like Rahmani. We all have our limits. Her taupe skirt is elegantly constructed, a slim sepal of sorts. Faroukh can't imagine she has two legs. It seems she would have one leg ending in a ball bearing. She glides away.

She hasn't looked at the little boys, not a glance.

"I'll walk you outside," says Blaise. "A breath of fresh air. I'm allowed."

They move forward, stumbling a little, it all happening too fast—as life does.

"So you're married," says Faroukh. The air has gotten icily colder.

"So are you."

"Children?"

"None. My wife—it is not possible." He doesn't elaborate. A woman that thin, that porcelained, Faroukh can imagine it. Auntie Nurjahan never had children either; her teenage anorexia had wreaked havoc with her potential. That had been the end of her brief marriage, too, as it happened. All that food she had made for Faroukh—she never ate more than a mouthful herself.

Faroukh said, meaning it, "She's exquisite. If you were to be married, I'd expect nothing less."

"If." Blaise is brave enough to repeat the word. "You're brave enough too, I see."

Faroukh lifts his chin. "Yes."

"I see your fine boys, I see your ring. So we both have what we wanted, don't we?"

How can Faroukh answer this? Even now he's not sure. Can one want more than one thing at a time? "You wanted children," he says.

"Oh," says Blaise. "*Pfahhh*," he says. "Well yes," he admits, "if you will. *Children*." He opens his hands, palms out, one near Jamesy, one near Matthias. "Children would have been worth it," he says more quietly. "It wasn't just to soothe my parents in their nightmare, nor to replace Monette or Cecile. Children for their own sake are worth it."

"Everything is worth it," says Faroukh. "Even the past is worth it."

"Your wife?" Blaise looks around. "She is with you? Or are you braving this reunion alone?" He looks suddenly eager, less tired. Even hungry.

Faroukh hoists Jamesy farther up his chest. He is a living breastplate laid against Faroukh's heart. He is asleep, but he is still protection. "The boys have two dads," he says. Not boasting, not defensively, not acidly. "We got married last fall in Cape Cod, where Jake maintains a second home. But we live in Minneapolis. Jake is a software engineer. I do what my baba eventually did: I manage properties. So I can be a stay-at-home dad."

"Oh," says Blaise. His arms open, shrugging a question into the air.

"His name is Jake," says Faroukh again. "But he's home with the dogs. I wanted to come alone. My father died last month—well, you know. When someone dies. The past is up for review. Anyway, I wanted to see this place. I didn't dare expect to see you. Not close up."

"But you came. You didn't come alone? You have a nanny at the hotel?"

"No." Faroukh laughs. "I'm managing. A lot of effort, no nanny. A kind of choice we made. So I'm never alone anymore. Even when I want to be."

"We can go out," says Blaise. "Later. You and I. We should. For old time's sake. Katrín will understand. She's very understanding. I give her her life, she gives me mine. . . ."

"Will she understand?" But Faroukh doesn't need to know if she really will or not. "I can't get together with you," he says. "I brought my children to be a reminder just in case I was tempted. They're in the way."

Jamesy is twitching in his sleep, Matthias is beginning to whine. "Can I carry one of them to the car?" asks Blaise. Matthias defies all expectation and allows Blaise to pick him up. Blaise and Faroukh step side by side off the granite ledge of the new performance center. Crystals of ice melt crush under the soles of their shoes.

Faroukh carries Jamesey, leaning in toward Blaise, singing a song the boys know, so they can hear it deep in their sleep, the way he deeply heard and will always remember his own baba's beloved Iranian songs. Faroukh sings, "'I gave my love a cherry without a stone. . . .'"

"I want you," says Blaise. "I always do. How can I say it so you know?"

Faroukh pauses, shivering. Wordlessly he takes Matthias back, balancing, balancing: a boy in each arm. Everything is modern now. In the brilliant snow, the buildings of Tupperneck stand out like architectural drawings lit from within. Students must be working in every room. Faroukh can see the stone steps leading up to the weighty porch that flanks three sides of Pierce. He turns back to answer Blaise, not knowing what he will say, just that he wants to say something. But at the sight of the famous man standing with two clenched fists against his breastbone, like the carving of a medieval knight readied for his own tomb, a carving still improbably upright, impossibly attractive and alive, Faroukh finds there is little in the library of all the lyrics he has ever heard to express what he now feels.

ABOUT THE AUTHORS

FRANCESCA LIA BLOCK is the recipient of the Margaret A. Edwards Award for lifetime achievement in young-adult literature. Her many acclaimed books for adults and young adults include *Dangerous Angels: The Weetzie Bat Books, Psyche in a Dress, Blood Roses, Quakeland, How to (Un)cage a Girl,* and *The Water & the Wild.* She lives in Los Angeles—the setting for much of her fiction—with her children.

JENNIFER FINNEY BOYLAN is the author of ten books, including the bestselling *She's Not There:*

A Life in Two Genders. A national spokeswoman on issues of gender, diversity, and civil rights, she has appeared on *The Oprah Winfrey Show*, *Larry King Live*, *Today*, and NPR's *Talk of the Nation*. Her new series for young readers, Falcon Quinn, will debut in 2010 from HarperCollins. A professor of English at Colby College, she lives in rural Maine with her spouse and two children.

EMMA DONOGHUE is a writer of novels, plays, and literary history. Best known for her historical fiction (*Slammerkin, Life Mask, The Woman Who Gave Birth to Rabbits*, and *The Sealed Letter*), she also writes contemporary fiction (*Stir-Fry, Hood, Touchy Subjects*, and *Landing*). Her first book for young adults was *Kissing the Witch: Old Tales in New Skins*. Born in Ireland, she now lives in London, Ontario, with her lover and two small children.

RON KOERTGE writes fiction for young adults and poetry for everybody. His latest young-adult novel is *Deadville* and his latest book of poems is *Fever*. He also teaches in Hamline College's MFA program for children's writing. A dedicated handicapper of thoroughbred racehorses, he can often be found near the saddling paddock at Santa Anita Race Track in Arcadia, California.

MARGO LANAGAN has been publishing novels and short stories for twenty years. Her collection of speculative fiction *Black Juice* won two World Fantasy Awards, was shortlisted for the *Los Angeles Times* Book Prize, and received a Michael L. Printz Honor. Her collection *Red Spikes* was made Book of the Year for Older Readers in the Children's Book Council of Australia Awards. Her most recent novel, *Tender Morsels*, also received a Michael L. Printz Honor. She lives in Sydney, Australia.

DAVID LEVITHAN is both an editor and author. When he isn't writing such novels as *Boy Meets Boy, The Realm of Possibility, Are We There Yet?*, and *Wide Awake*, he works as executive editorial director of Scholastic Press Fiction, Multimedia Publishing, and PUSH, the young-adult imprint that he founded. His novel *Nick & Norah's Infinite Playlist*, coauthored with Rachel Cohn, recently became a major motion picture. He lives in Hoboken, New Jersey.

GREGORY MAGUIRE is the author of a dozen children's novels, including *What-the-Dickens*, and six novels for adults. The sequence known as the Wicked Years includes *Wicked* (which inspired the Broadway musical of the same name), *Son of a Witch*, and *A Lion Among Men*. His articles and reviews have appeared in *OutTraveler*, *The New York Times Book Review*, *Commonweal*, and *Ploughshares*. He lives primarily in New England with his husband, the painter Andy Newman, and their three children.

JULIE ANNE PETERS is the author of fifteen books for young adults and children. Her young-adult novel *Luna* was a National Book Award finalist and an ALA Best Book for Young Adults. Her other books about gender-queer youth include *Keeping You a Secret*, *Far from Xanadu*, *grl2grl: short fictions*, and *Rage: A Love Story*. A member of SCBWI, Pen America, the Authors Guild, and the Colorado Authors' League, she lives in Lakewood, Colorado, with her partner, Sherri Leggett.

ARIEL SCHRAG is the author of the graphic novels *Awkward*, *Definition*, *Potential*, and *Likewise*. *Potential* was nominated for an Eisner Award and is currently being developed into a feature film. She is the editor—and a contributor to—the anthology *Stuck in the Middle: Seventeen Comics from an Unpleasant Age* and was a writer for seasons three and four of the Showtime series *The L Word*. She lives in Los Angeles.

ERIC SHANOWER is the two-time Eisner Award–winning cartoonist of the graphic novel series Age of Bronze, an ongoing retelling of the Trojan War. His past work includes the Oz graphic novel series, many other comic books, and illustrations for television, magazines, and children's books, two of which he also wrote. He lives in San Diego, California, with his partner.

WILLIAM SLEATOR is the author of more than thirty young-adult books, most of them science fiction and thrillers. His many awards include the California Young Readers Medal—voted by teenagers—for *Interstellar Pig*. Until recently, he lived in a small village near the Cambodian border in Thailand with his partner of eighteen years, Lep. If you think this means "Fingernail" might be based on a true story, he says, you're right! "Fingernail" is dedicated to Lep, who died in December 2008 at the age of forty-seven.

JACQUELINE WOODSON is a recipient of the Margaret A. Edwards Award for lifetime achievement in young-adult literature. Her novel *Miracle's Boys* received both the Coretta Scott King and *Los Angeles Times* Book Awards, while both *Locomotion* and *Hush* were National Book Award finalists. Her novels *Show Way*, *Feathers*, and *After Tupac and D Foster* were all selected as Newbery Honor Books. She lives in Brooklyn, New York, with her partner and two children.